To all the
Friends I Killed

LYS
www.lysforlag.com
Editorial office: redaktion@lysforlag.com
Project manager: Sofi Tegsveden Deveaux
Cover and book design: Sofi Tegsveden Deveaux

To all the
Friends I Killed

JOSHUA KENT BOOKMAN

LYS

To all my friends

1.

We were playing a new version. Text and seek. Kajsa would text me the coordinates of where she was at, say, a cemetery. I'd show up to the cemetery, she'd be behind the trees, see me, text me another location. She'd already be at a Japanese restaurant, food on the table, waiting with two chopsticks.

Kajsa was my sister, but someone I met later in life, after college, when some high school friends had moved, and others lost touch. She acted just like a sister, loyal, and if we had fought, it was temporary. I never considered her a friend, even if that's what strangers thought she was. The most remarkable of our lives had to be elevated to family.

She drew on the chopsticks. Little hashmarks with her fingernails, faux characters that said something wise, not Buddha wise or Shinto wise but sister wise, like, «days were better spent outside in the rush of the morning fifteen minutes before lunch.» She had a thing for little moments, or periods of time, time that wasn't labeled ordinarily. «Early morning» or «late morning» was 7:47, or 11:49, those specific times, that's what defined us. I liked this because I had a Swiss friend obsessed with watches, typical, stereotypical, yes, but it reinforced the point that it wasn't the precision of time that Kajsa liked. It was the momentary flashes of time that no one else thought to celebrate.

Like the two minutes before ordering. Impatience was the

virtue, because as soon as I'd be hungry, that's when she'd say «don't you like that feeling?»

«What feeling?» I asked.

«Where you know you're hungry, but can't order, because the server is with someone else.»

«How is that a good feeling.»

«It's the two minute anticipation,» she said. «You'll know the waiter'll be there in just a minute or two but have to endure it anyway, it makes you that much edgier.»

The endurance of impatience, another inscription she slashed on the chopsticks. This time though she took the two bamboo knives in her fingertips and scraped little papercliplike indentations into the table.

Kajsa had sea glass eyes, hazy and brittle. I had thought my eyes were prettier, but when she was upset, they dazzled the room with unusual tints of color, ocean blue, bottle green. My eyes couldn't do that. They were marked with crimson.

We would order, at last. Her endurance her thing, impatience my thing. There was no shame in it since she smiled at me when I hailed the waiter. I couldn't wait any longer.

«A beer,» I said.

«A beer?» she said.

«A beer, two?» the waiter asked.

«One beer,» Kajsa said.

Then the waiter would leave and she'd start the game all over again. Why, if I was so hungry, did I not order drinks in the first place, fifteen minutes ago, and then be ready to place the order.

We'd fight about nothing, really. That was why she was my sister. Friends would fight and I would need space, for at least a day or two. But our arguments never lasted longer than a couple hours. Once I got so mad I shut the door on her and then she just sat outside, slumped against the wall until she decided I had brooded long enough and kicked my door open. She has — siblings had higher courage in diffusing one's worst emotions.

Six minutes later, Kajsa would ask for the specials, the back list of the waiter's notebook, scribbled in Japanese. I'd let her order because she'd struggle to repeat what was said, rapidfire.

After the minutes of bickering, we'd sit in silence. The long wait before the order again. We'd order, and then more silence. Kajsa took this as an opportunity to play another game, texting me from the kitchen of the restaurant. Somehow she had snuck in.

«What's the opposite of butter?»

The answer wasn't obvious, say, olive oil. It'd be a sequence of answers. I'd have to think of the situation. We were at a Japanese restaurant, so it wasn't an issue of pure obvious choice but aesthetics. The Japanese way of arranging the plate, or the choice of color.

Butter was yellow. Like the shiso leaf, the particular color of the green leaf, the particular color of butter could matter. But maybe she wasn't thinking of color theory, that was too much my reasoning. The opposite of yellow was purple, like the sour plum, the ones that you could get in a jar, pickled, rumpled skins rolling against purple salt water, but purple was overused, so she meant violet. Violet, the faded color of purple, the intense color of purple, these both were legitimate, because she was forcing me to play the game deliberately, slowly, thinking of all the possible combinations of what butter could and couldn't be. Violet was her sister, so, the opposite of a sister was me, her brother!

Again, it's not that Kajsa couldn't have had siblings from childhood. If someone asked me to tell the truth, I'd say yes, Kajsa has two siblings. There was nothing shameful about vocalizing the strength of our relationship.

Nothing in the world was as creative as our games, as fulfilling as this back and forth between us that wasn't covered in magazines or television scripts. How could it be? Since we were the only ones who knew the game!

I need to admit though, that the games didn't last much longer.

Kajsa was struck by a car. We were walking from the cemetery to the nearby park. I had wanted to go on the swingset but she said that was childish. Even though the week before she had begged me for the same thing, and never did I say it was childish of her, the older sister, to suggest something so crude and unimaginative to do as limit our fun to the preschool park swing. I didn't like the idea, and as we were walking to the park, run jogging at this point, I had pushed her into the street. There was a little street between the cemetery and the park. There weren't cars. But this time there were cars, one car, I had pushed her into the street with that car.

I report this like that's how sisters end up, four years later and they're gone, but to this day I don't understand what happened. I tried calling the police, no, I don't have a legitimate thing to report. Thing? She needed help, an ambulance. They asked me to list every detail of what happened but I couldn't because I admit I was in shock and no I hadn't intended to do anything even if at that moment in time I was mad and at this moment in time I am still mad, because no one had loved me as much as Kajsa. The police told me to, again, retell the part between the cemetery and the park and I couldn't because it was too much. The days just kept going, each day an officer would call and I would manage to say something that would help recreate the situation but I didn't want to recreate anything. I wanted to pretend it never happened or at least move on from what wasn't my fault, since we were both at fault. We were the sun of our lives and two weeks later, it was over.

2.

I wrote my plan on an index card. At the top, in permanent marker, a quote by the famous figure skater Jurgen Klistof. He said in the second act of the performance, always land. The first, you could stumble. I took this as reality. I stumbled. But I would land.

My hand shook as I was figuring out whether I should first write «pack,» or «bank.» I had determined I would get a job. The job couldn't require too much documentation. I couldn't flag the police. The sergeant in charge said to call if there was a problem, or something I remembered. I couldn't remember the order in which he told me these things which is why I was making very sure I wrote an exact order to «pack» and «bank.»

An hour earlier I had bought a one-way ticket to France. I was going to get a seasonal job, there wouldn't be a need to open a new bank account, it would all be underreported earnings. Grapes was the third item on the index card.

After I determined the order of my plan, I left. I left my apartment. I left most of my clothes. I kept Kajsa's sweatshirt, the one that was way too big for me, too big for her too. I wore it to the airport.

It was a small thing, to wear your sibling's clothing during childhood. A very direct way to share, and it was convenient. But for me it was a conscious decision, since we didn't live together. I had to go over, talk about our day, the news, something trivial, and then sneak into her closet, grab something that wasn't mine. This habit took time to make it look real. That was the challenge of not-so-strictly-speaking siblings. But as will become obvious, I like challenges. After all this time, they still only give me the keyboard for an hour.

When I landed, I wasn't sure if that was a good thing. It had happened so quickly, closing my eyes on the plane, six, seven hours later I was somewhere new. I knew, yes, this was Europe, this was a country that would be familiar. How familiar I wasn't certain, but I knew I would be very alone, without family. The grapes were to act as my companions.

trois.

At the airport exit, I saw family shout, smile, hug their relatives. That long hug, by the girl in front of me. I tried to feel it too, as if her mother were also hugging me. I stood there, waiting for the invitation. Her mother shot a look, of fear, of confusion. I looked at her, I said «*bonjour*.» She said «*bonjour*» back and then grabbed her daughter's hand, striding away from me.

I tried this one more time, with the limo driver and his sign «ROUSQIEU.» If I were French I'd be a Rousqieu, for sure. I waved at him but he did not wave back. I saw a policeman leaning against the railing. He turned his body and then adjusted his lacquered black hat.

I walked over towards the buses, where there was a large map of Bordeaux. There were intersecting red lines, street routes, points of interest, exclamation points, I couldn't see what was the point of this map. I hopped on the first bus that arrived, in line behind a family of four and a couple, holding hands.

At a certain point the bus got us into the city, and I stepped off. I was tired of sitting and I thought if I was going to jail, I might've well as seen the opposite, a city.

It will be clear later that I might go to jail, or that I am in jail. Life wasn't over just because I was a bit insane.

I wandered down a street that had a row of boutiques.

Collections of antiques, chandeliers mostly, and bronze molds, seals for hot wax. It seemed like an odd assortment of possessions that someone had kept, hoarded, and then one day turned into an idea for a store. There was a passerby next to me, with a puzzled look.

«Crazy, right?» I said. I thought it'd be nice to share what I was thinking. Something else that would be gone, too, people to express my opinions. Couldn't hurt.

The passerby stuffed his hands deep into his trench coat pockets and stepped into the store.

I tried to follow him but I stopped and turned around. I kept looking at more boutiques, stepping into one, then stepping out, unsure if I was seeing blood or dirt or if it was some other crimson hue. At the end of the block, a glass display of wines. Gold bottles that glinted every so often, a sparkle here and there with the movement of the clouds. I walked inside to speak with the store owner.

«*Bonjour,*» I said.

«*Bonjour,*» he said. He did not look up.

«Yes, *bonjour,*» I said. «May I ask where those bottles're from?»

The man, with small glasses, and a cane, pointed east.

«Sauternes,» he said.

«Thank you,» I said. I wrote it down, misspelling probably, and began to look at the bottles more closely. Even next to them, there was the sense of nectar, and the color of yellow apricots.

«Those you may also be interested in,» he said. He used his cane to point at two bottles in the corner. «Sainte-Croix-du-Mont. Not as expensive, just as delicious.»

A policeman walked through the door. He tipped his hat to the store owner.

«Oh,» I said. «Cool. Why?»

He adjusted his glasses. «Poor taste.»

«Oh.»

«Not Sainte-Croix. People without taste.»

I thanked him and smiled, but dashed out, afraid. Maybe that was part of moving on, focusing on other things that were bothering me. I already knew what was expensive. The cost of absence, for example. It was relieving to hear someone who could distinguish quality regardless of price, and a village that could taste its quality without high price was a place worthwhile to know, a place where I could forget specific relationships and to avoid the officer.

Could I go to Sainte-Croix-du-Mont? There, I'd be safe to explore this 'just as delicious' idea. I could know what it'd be like to live in the shadow of something more expensive. I wasn't as wealthy, but being surrounded by it was just as memorable.

The bus depot was a grid of gray and black shelters. The sun had set and all the color oozed out of the city. At one end of the station there was a group of kids just stepping off a bus, from their village I had imagined, spilling out onto the street like ants, filing towards their destination. Their oversized backpacks, like thoraxes, insectly proportioned. On the other end, there was an elderly man with too-big sneakers, leaning against a bike rack, tapping his fingers against the rubber wheels. I had approached him and asked where the Sainte-Croix-du-Mont bus was, and he shoved me behind him. He wanted to be first.

I got on the bus and began my trip, taking up two seats, one for my backpack, smaller, not French, but safe, elementary school — a zipper and colored pencils, crayons — colors to soothe me. And one seat for me, taking a deep breath. I had landed.

As the city faded away, we swerved through little villages, a group of twenty of us becoming seventeen, then fourteen, then twelve. I liked this game, it had reminded me of what Kajsa and I used to play, I didn't need to give her up completely. I grabbed my backpack, to write the numbers down, 20, 17, 14, 12, new numbers for a new game. I fumbled with the zipper, shaking it open, seeing the empty contents, my passport and the index card. I couldn't find my notebook, and if I couldn't write it down, I'd be stuck with the old game. My heart was beating more, I sat with her sweatshirt still on me, soaked with sweat. I turned to the window and a bird smashed towards me.

It had pierced the window and reverberated throughout the bus. No one else reacted. If it had died on impact, it'd be on the floor, but it was not there. I looked towards the front of the bus, seeing if the driver had a winged creature on its shoulder. It wasn't there either. I closed my eyes and told myself this was a test. I remembered long ago, when I was a kid, I had watched a television show where young warriors were told by their great spiritual masters that they would be undergoing a long journey. The journey wouldn't be obviously labeled. Some days it would feel like the master had abandoned him, but that too was a test. I thought that maybe this was all full circle, I just had to trust it. I placed my backpack on my lap. Without the energy to write I began whispering the word test, test, test, drifting off.

quatre.

I heard faint church bells, the last of the evening. I turned my neck to the right window, and saw night. To my left, my backpack on the seat. My belongings were still there.

I hopped off the bus, the last of the passengers. It was a main road, next to a restaurant that was closed, and houses with the shutters bolted up. I saw a curved path, upwards to higher ground. How high I wanted to know. The wind howled.

When I started the incline, it hit me this was not a city, not even a big town. The sky, completely open, a roll of soft felt fabric stretched over miles. The stars, bright white and proud, citizens of the village. They hovered over me, washing away the voices I was hearing.

«*Bonsoir,*» she said.

A woman in front of me held a shovel.

«*Bonsoir,*» I said.

«A bit late to be looking,» she said. She had graying hair, but it was still in parts black, glimmering from the streetlight and the dance of spotted moths.

I didn't know what I could say. Looking for what, I wasn't sure. But I had better be honest. It was an opportunity to tell someone the truth.

«Yes, I'm looking for work,» I said.

The woman put down her shovel and reached for the pocket of her overalls. She grabbed a pencil.

«Your name, then.»

«Jeppe,» I said.

«Last name?» she asked.

«No, first name.» She scribbled the letter Y. «No, it starts with a J. A bit complicated.» I laughed, nervous, but she didn't laugh or smile back.

«Very well,» she said. «Be here tomorrow for a bit more paperwork. Seven. You'll start the day after.»

«Thank you… really, I am very grateful.»

«Seven tomorrow,» she said. «Good night.»

«Good night,» I said. She picked up her shovel and continued to fix whatever path she was working on. I tiptoed up the hill, looking for a place to rest my backpack, away from streetlights. I saw a cemetery further up, but she must've seen me.

«There's a little house in the back,» she shouted. «You can stay there till the others arrive.»

5.

I would stay in that little house, a château I would get to know like a second home. It was a spot that would extend into memories of other places, and complicate the idea that we only live in one place at a time. Because I don't live in one place.

It is standard procedure that I chew pills in the afternoon. This is normal, and shouldn't deter anyone from thinking otherwise substantial ideas about the ways we live, the limits we accept and don't accept about ourselves and others.

Unfortunately I stayed up all night and needed a sedative to be coherent. Both last night and the night I'm recounting I hadn't slept, I had that much stress, replaying events, recording my actions. We live in one place at a time, but the impressions of many remodel what's considered the present. I could describe it like fog, which is both ground and atmosphere, or as an open vault, where memories, like prized possessions, never get entirely stored away.

For weeks after my trip to France I had laid in bed. I was at a youth hostel in Boston, hiding, staring at the ceiling. How one plane ride could change things.

«Hey,» he said. A guy above me was trying to get my attention. We shared bunk beds, but I ignored him.

I missed Kajsa. See, she was a milestone. People say after

childhood, your partner, that's the most important relationship of your life, the most difficult decision you make.

«Hello, I'm talking to you,» he said.

But I'd argue until I was bloody crimson that there was no recognition for the wisest friends we chose as adults. If a partner died, and that's all you had, you were crippled. Or if all you had was a child, that was worse. But a friend, a couple of good friends, ones that lasted at least ten years, a decade or more, well even maybe a century. Now that would certainly distribute the weight of death. Then you'd get to laugh by a factor of x friends, and then it was a village of people, not just the one person nudging you through life's volatility. That was the milestone of choosing a sibling when you were older. We all had childhood anchors, but no one thought to create one for your adult life. No one thought that it was a major success to find a sibling of your own volition, who loved you just as much as a biological one. Or maybe even loved you more than a biological one ever could.

«Hey are you listening?»

I turned to face him.

Kajsa had not prepared me for the aftermath. New people vying for my attention, like those snack vendors at baseball games. «Geeet your hot dogs! Geeet your aduuult siblings! Last you a lifetime!»

And police, like gargoyles, protruding everywhere. What was the point of developing a theory if she was dead?

I understood the implications. I killed my dearest friend. But consequence could be twain, beautiful and horrible, just like France. Marie the good, the vineyards, the land, and Marie the bad, the cheater, the too sweet.

A month must've passed from the time I checked into the ward, the hostel. I didn't know whether the other hostelgoers thought I was Hungarian, or Italian, maybe Argentinian, but I liked to pretend. Like the guy above me, on the bunk bed, I messed with him.

«So you is a wondering of me,» I said.

I was realizing that here, everyone's tone was so positive, and fake.

«Wondering of you?» he asked.

I grabbed his arm and dragged him to the cafeteria. A windowless, a skyless, sweet prison.

So seriously positive, that they made you feel that you were the crazy one, when in reality it was them who were going to copy your theory after it was written.

«Why *je* still here.»

I loosened my French between countries. I wondered if he'd notice.

I think he thought I was cool, that we could be friends.

«I'm here to sell *immaginazione*,» I said, twirling into an Italian. I was now, I think, pretending to be a tourist in my own homeland.

«What language is that?» he asked. «It's so beautiful. Is that Sp-panish?»

Moments like this were so frustrating. I wished I still had Kajsa to intervene, to explain why I was so strange, why I wanted to be a musician.

«I always wanted to learn Sp-panish. For business, you know, for my job.»

People needed art — that is, sensations. Touch, taste, smell, hear. See, art was the only thing that let us safely imagine a better future. But look at this cafeteria! I bet you every baked good, heck every person here was made in a facility that shared a production line with soy, nuts and gluten. I bet you the coffee was a deal cut by the hostel with a mega conglomerate. See, all we imagined was swiftly competitive, even our food was a competition we could rationalize, or sell, by the minute. That left no room for the evolution of our humanity, which was on a time-scale bigger than a quarterly report, or a year. Ten years — a decade — now that was a start, at least that was why I thought sisters and brothers weren't labeled ordinarily by time, because we were forced to eat with them for more than a year. I thought a civilization would die without siblingy long term investment, in all its senses. That's why my chosen sister was such a big milestone.

Kajsa would've told me to look at time — a month gone by — and say Jeppe, wake up. A month is longer than it takes a gosling's neck to change color. She would say that about work — employment, a new chance, your neck's chance. I giggled a bit, thinking how she'd cheer me up with silly rhymes. She was right. My next chance would work out, if I let it, so I dropped my voice box to an American English and relented. «I need a job.»

«I thought you were on a tourist's visa,» he said.

«I am,» I said. «From Milan. Using my computer skills and *immaginazione* to get a job,» I said.

I bowed, and hurried to my room, waving a goodbye. He didn't get the joke.

I opened my door to the clacked air of rotting grapes. A homeland in reverse, with broken feelings, which I refused to reject just yet.

That was the unusual thing about France, the word *air* used to describe a feeling, an atmosphere. My rain boots slept in the corner of my room. The *air* of melancholy. They were a forest hue lighter now, covered in dirt and dust, a twig sunken into the sole of the boots. I hadn't washed them.

I hadn't washed Kajsa's sweatshirt either, even after all these months. It helped settle things for me, keeping some part of the relationship dirty. Not everything of course, was kept like that. Some things had to be pristine. Earlier this morning I was dreaming about Kajsa, staring up at her old apartment. I stared also at the clouds, the cars, the sidewalk. Passersbys on the street shot quick glances, wondering if I was looking to rent or just lost. I looked up again. Her window sill had a scrap of birchwood laying on it. She thought it was unusual, because most people put a tulip, or rose, or something clichélike.

«Hey, Jeppe?»

I turned to see the hostelgoer. Gosh, how did he know my name. Did I tell him?

«Do you want to go to Provincetown with me? I'm catching the next bus.»

«I don't know,» I said.

«No?» He laughed. «But you're just sitting here all day,» he said.

«I'm writing lyrics,» I said.

«Okay, how about you write some lyrics on the bus. The view will inspire you.»

«What view?» I said.

He put his arm over my shoulder.

«Imagine the most beautiful view of the ocean.» Of course

I saw vines and I couldn't just shake off my visions. Although I could try to escape them, just in case the police were working for Marie.

«Fine,» I said. «Only if you shut up and let me write the whole time.»

Yeah, we were not cliché. But it was frightening. We were going to Provincetown, a place without a friend, and French police. At last I'd be far away from Inspector Mauriac. There'd be no way to find me. This was a test, a new test.

vines, not snow, or sanguine,
what a sister could see,
what a sister could blee',
what a sister could be.

The church bells sung through the bus' windows. Alone, I kept writing and rewriting the lyrics. Yes, I struggled to find a sibling in France, but maybe that was because of the grape leaves, and the officer. It was impossible to lead a new life when I was the thorn that followed.

The fleas that batted and bazzed what stuck,
The rot of the grapes

My mind, the detective. He could rip the leaves out.

Vines were so unusual — the time was new, relying on clouds — relying on rain to say whether I could work. Most phones were set to a twelve hour or twenty four hour clock, and then there were watches, laptop reminders, alarms. But there was an ancient tradition to wake up, open the door and tilt one's neck towards the sky. I was not ready to give that up.

But of course that was a bit of a lie to myself.
*the leaves (*les feuilles*) bitter amok,*

In truth (in fact, if I'm using that *en fait*, and making it my own, what, arrest me for franglais?), the honest truth was the extent of my loneliness. I had no friends. I couldn't, they'd just be a spy.

It wasn't that I struggled to know that I was lonely. I could not, for example, I could not see why this guy wanted to catch the bus with me. In the United States it was better to go into the situation alone, than dead. Maybe he'd report me, or better yet, kill me himself.

But in France, I learned, or maybe I was still learning, it was better to express your feelings to others, however contradictory, than be alone. It's like Marie openly admitted how she felt about her crimes, my crimes. Crimes not just committed to other people, but forced upon myself. I was a self-convict.

But there wasn't much life left, if I turned myself in. Solitude was safer. Which is why when I saw the view of the ocean, and the Cape, glowing from the bus' window frame, I knew, I knew there might be something to this town.

The view, it was like the thwapping of a picnic blanket when you first arrived at a park.

I had no previsions of it, that was what I liked. Just looking at the ocean, staring, its infinity, I didn't know if I was supposed to expect chaos, a small town, a beach town, a village, a seasonal city, whatever the descriptions I had heard, I ignored them all, I never assumed what I was going to see and feel.

All I knew was I knew no one. I wanted to say goodbye to my new friend, but in truth it wasn't good. Why did people say

«Goodbye» anyways? In French, *au revoir* «to the re-see.» The hostelgoer and I were not going to see each other again.

«We could exchange Instagrams,» he said.

It was not good, but bad. Like the definition of terrific, negative and positive, it was context, or *terrible*, like badass, an uncompromising, impressive person, an impressive bye. I was using bad in a flipped sense.

«Bad bye,» I said.

It was that simple, a quick connection. And then he was off to the beach.

So he was someone I'd never meet again, or maybe yes. I didn't know how it would work, maybe that was the thrilling part.

I think that was part of my new purpose, to make friends, not siblings, particularly ones that I wouldn't murder.

«Name?» the agent said. To clarify, a real estate agent. But what was real about the business of ownership?

«Jeppe...» I said, stammering. Marie had asked my name, and it had not ended to plan.

«Right.» She scribbled down «Yep» on her little notebook pad. I thought for a second she was a police officer.

«So what kind of place're you looking for?»

Her office was spare. A single painting, of Dalí's grandson, and a window sill tulip. No crop of soil, no bottles of wine, no shovel.

«A little garden, ideal. Or just, a place outside.»

«This is the outside, hon.» She wrote «particular.»

«I... I know,» I said. «I want a place where I can, call it my own space.»

«Right. So, a one bedroom is it?»

«Nn. — No. It doesn't have to be, but I understand if —

«My dear, you won't find much here.»

«But the reas—

«At this point in the season your options are your options.»

«Meaning?» I asked.

«You...» She stopped to compose herself. «You may want to consider what is your most important priority.» She adjusted her dress, a romper, which had big white rhododendrons on it, and to match, a sunflower in her hat. She grabbed the flower and put it against her nose, breathing in, then crumpling it. She tossed it into the trash can.

«A space to play.» «To write. My music... I'm... I'm a songwriter.» I lied to her. Again, a half lie. I composed songs, I just didn't share that fact because I didn't mean music in the conventional sense. No one had time to recognise the music of our everyday voices. I liked doctors for that reason. The patient's struggle to make sense of pain was itself a lyric. We just had to listen to our own pain more.

«Right... beautiful.» «Well, there's one place.» She glanced towards her computer screen and turned the monitor to show me. Police log 1037.

«Maybe it's not the most ideal situation, but why don't you take a look?»

«Ye—

«Yep, I wrote it down. A nice name.»

«J—

«Oh, and welcome to PTown. You will love it here.»

sept.

The grape sugar suffused the air, and the château's archway door popped with the morning's first light. Before I knew it, I was outside, rushing to make my first impression. In front of me were ten or so workers, with a rotating wheel of introductions, double kisses, handshakes, and a half cup of coffee.

«Hi,» a woman said.

A woman, Catherine, six feet tall, put up her hand as a hello. She had dark forest boots, chestnut braids, black leggings. I waved back. I then introduced myself to the two Romanian workers, the one Italian, the three French. At this point no one seemed distinguishable. They all wore similar green boots, footwear that would be dirty within a week's time, hats that shaded their faces, which had no makeup, no sunscreen.

It had been a long time since I had to make friends. I cringe even thinking of that word now, because really they were all acquaintances. Colleagues, co-workers, etc., these were all words used to distance ourselves from people we didn't know, we didn't trust. It was the ever-expanding list of categories adults created to feel more comfortable with the fact they did not know the very people with whom they spent their days.

We trudged into the fields of grapes. The vines were vast, rows that blurred into little hills of light green orbs that dotted the landscape like flowers. Never had I worked a place so close to the Earth, where the soil around me, the sun, it all wrapped you into the feeling of belonging to something beyond you. Maybe it didn't matter what I had done. Yes, I was still taking my pills. No, Provincetown I had not started to. I managed without that type of help for a while.

«Clip here,» the proprietor said, pointing at the tip of the stem. She cut off a bunch to demonstrate, plucking only the ripest, the roundest. I copied what she did. I made sure nothing she did I didn't not do. I couldn't be reprimanded, or worse, fired on the first day of work. I considered myself lucky that she hadn't asked for any documents from me, at least not yet. I was going to tell her that I preferred cash, but I wanted to wait. A week at least to let her trust me.

By mid-morning there was a snack pause, just like preschool. We sat on the hill at the top of one of the vines, sprawled out, as our boss floated around us.

«Coffee, *chocolatine*?» she asked. She folded back wax paper to reveal studs of dark chocolate.

I pulled apart the croissant, loose threads of wheat and butter melting onto my fingers. This was the first thing I had eaten since the bus depot. I had forgotten what it was like to enjoy something, not just around other people, but with them.

I put my gloves back on and got back to work, that hour alongside one of the Frenchmen, Elias. As we went vine by vine, and the sun rose higher into the sky, towards its zenith, I realized how hot it was getting. The sunburn was obvious in Elias' irises, already a faded blue, but even more translucent from the heat.

We stopped shortly thereafter, walking back to the château,

the large house nearby to where I was sleeping. We took off our boots, letting them and our socks dry under the sun as we prepared ourselves to eat. In the garden was a long stone table, set with twelve plates, forks and knives, cloth napkins. Lunch, the languor of our bodies, an exquisite sequence of dishes, rillettes, baguettes, melon, vin rouge from 2015 and 2016 harvests, a carrot beef stew, four fromages, a galette bretonne, and coffee. Since Kajsa was lost I couldn't help but miss the royal delight of the moment, wanting something grand and sweet to digest the pain, lingering before we had to return to the day at hand.

The afternoon burned quickly, clearing the vines at a rapid pace, no more than five minutes per row, blistering through each clip without much chatter. We had finished quickly, but this time had taken the *fourgon*, the big white van, back to the château. I sat next to Gaëtan, I think 73, 74, who, like Elias, had sunburnt eyes, but they looked like glaciers. I saw Kajsa in the ice, something Gaëtan was trying to say to me, I knew it, although I couldn't understand much of what he was saying. His eyes glowed with her, a stare that said for me to admit it. She was not as important as you think, she was just someone to care about before you met the love of your life. I was about to say yes, I killed you, but I had shaken off his glances, only to turn back to him. The ice was melting but she was still there, solid. In the half shadows of the van his eyes pierced through me pale azure reliquaries.

8.

Welcome to PTown, *d'accord*, sure, air of the new.

I admit, France was a terrible idea, in fact. I went to a random country and expected to ditch my feelings. Find myself. *Oui*, I did find something out, it was that I grew up in a society that thought my search for a sister was crazy. What a wonderful realization that I was trapped in a place that tried every minute to swallow my sense of joy, unless that joy meant money or marriage. I was absolutely determined to make my life not just about Ms.

It may have been easier to proceed with my life in a fairly linear fashion, Sainte-Croix-du-Mont, then Massachusetts, but that's not how we proceed when we're reconciling our past. If I was going to make sense of it all, I had to accept that it was more valuable to position the past within the confines of the present. I may live in a hospital, but that's not how I see it. I live in the only place that tolerates time out of order.

I didn't know what exactly my life would be, but the United States would change, and I would change it, even if it meant I'd die in the process. My report said suicidal tendencies, but I think the doctor meant martyr, visionary, assassinated by social convention.

In one of our scheduled classes, we were allowed to imagine ourselves writing to a foreign government or institution. For some of my classmates, who go unnamed (patient-patient confidentiality), they had chosen peculiar institutions, like the National British Museum, pretending to be an Egyptian archeologist, recovering stolen objects, or the National Brazilian Repository of Insects, pretending to be butterflies, but I imagined writing a postcard to the French Academy. I figured it might be more receptive to a non-chronological series of events.

To: Académie Française,

May you accept my travels as literature. It is not an accident I'm back in the United States. Senses, Experience, that is what you teach to me, it is for sure a good thing.

Sincerely,
Jeppe

I had to be a poet, not a novelist, for lack of a better analogy. To kill lines, and make meaning through silence. I was going to be paid not per word, like actors or yes, novelists, but per lack of word. I'd admit my crimes, as long as the sentences were short. Did you know at the height of a very successful actor's career, he can make $4000 a word. Again, $4000. How could I possibly make a living if we were built on mass content? Yes, and the award for the least amount of space in society goes to...

I was remembering how lost I felt traveling, and how I clutched onto her clothing. It was time to be honest. Get rid of old clothing. Siblings told the truth, and since I had to wash her sweater, I... I was now Kajsa, I had to become the truthful one.

There were some things about America that I had to disinfect, before like a grape, it rotted and spread.

I rented a bike, roamed all over town, and found a laundromat. I stunk.

I couldn't rely on her to be the one comforting me. Today I would try to be my own older sister, even if I didn't know how.

The laundromat was scented. I may have smelled like a hostel carpet, but this was different, worse. Strong, CVS- or Walmartlike, fluorescent lights, loud final spins, it was trumpet blood. Those last minutes I couldn't breathe. But no, a sister would've told me to love those minutes.

I saw the store across the street, a boutique painted green, yellow and black wood tiles. Its walls were sunken, slumped next to a wood chest, a trash can, a military truck. It looked like me, jumbled, eclectic, wishing to be better curated.

I walked over. I saw the owner, a woman in her fifties. She was not like me.

«What would you like?» she said. An island tone.

«A snack,» I said, scoutin' the jackfruit and pineapple sodas.

«The chicken'n rice?» she said. She tried to hype it, and sell more. At least that was my attitude. But the analysis wasn't necessary. An accent hit me.

«Mm, just a snack,» I said. I saw Jamaican porridge and fried foods in the window box.

«You work here?» she said. She glanced at me. Her eyes were ready, briefly dear.

«Yeah till the winter.» I lied. Still no job.

«That's whata I was sayin',» she said, sweeping the floor, the wood tiles outside now a brighter green n yellow n a black. I was noticing her broom magic.

«So the chicken 'n' rice?» she said.

«I don't got much cash,» I said. «Quarters from the laundry.»

People were whipping out their clothes, quick detergent in, quarters slamming, elderly men dozing off by the radiators, barely away of the Jamaican radio beats.

She pulled out a round ball, an oil orb.

«Fifty cents,» she said.

«What's this called?» I asked.

«Fried dumplin,» she said.

I thanked her, but walkin' outside with the dumplin its starchy cassava potato mm not sur' the starch be filling me and the oil printed to my fingers, my ribs.

I was a bit of Jamaica, a bit of the US. The Cape breeze and detergent air mixed, scattered between two Outer Cape realities. The porch rocked a way from the laundromat, the thickness of fake scents diluted. My idea of Massachusetts was being reformed, by accents, by flavors, by the Cape's ocean-touching Caribbean. I didn't know her name, but her boutique was pushing me away from moneyed analysis into oil orb territory. The waves I saw here weren't defined by its oceans, and $35 parking passes I saw on my bike ride in, and sex. Tidality wasn't just a logistical exercise. Tidality was the frayed peripheries of life, comforted by the ritual flow of surprises. I liked this boutique and maybe I'd work here.

9.

The fake estate agent wasn't wrong. The house she suggested was… sort of like if a ladder had been set where the front door should've. A big antique window. Loose shingles. Streaks of sunflower yellow paint. *C'était joli*. It's pretty.

Inside, there was a kettle. I flicked it, it was a ping sound, like a kettle. That was okay. I flicked it again, just to make sure it wasn't a siren.

It was quite pretty — porcelain copper. It also had a pfing noise, ping, pfing. The sound echoed off the kitchen tiles, light from the window clouds shadowing.

There was an open beer can. The liquid dripped out, on the floor, I touched the floor. It was a floral beer, chrysanthemum aromas that drifted up as I swirled my toe in its puddle. I'd take the apartment.

When I walked outside, I met Foska. She bumped into me, I didn't expect us to start a conversation.

I hoped it wasn't about how much the place cost. Of all the listings the agent showed, few were cheap. Live in the shadow of something more expensive, the wine merchant had said.

«Apologies,» I said.

«What?» Foska said.

«I said I'm sorry,» I said.

«No you said apologies. Like a weird British person.»

«Bloody habit, I guess.» Ha, bloody. It was no longer lying, it was poetic.

«Yeah, a weird habit,» she said.

«You use weird a lot.»

«I've used it twice.»

Foska was strange. She was combative, rude, but she was also the rare person I met in town who paid attention to what I said, my choice of words, the tone, whether I repeated something, if there was any lyricality to my expressions. A friend, maybe, but later a regret of who she knew. A tour, yes *un tour à chacun son tour*. Everybody had his turn.

That was the challenge of introductions. Everyone said make a good impression, but that was poor advice. If you were too polite, or she was too polite, no one got a sense of who the person was. No one ever wrote a song about how affable and respectful someone was, for good reason.

«What's your name, sire?»

«Jeppe,» I said.

«Is that American?»

«It's Scandinavian for Jacob,» I said. «My parents were weird.»

«Right, weird, like I said. Anyways, got to go. Bye for now.»

Foska hopped on her bike, tapping the bell with just her fingernails, loud enough that only I could hear it.

dix.

I laid in bed, Gaëtan's eyes piercing through me. My whole body, scratched from thorns, coated with dried sweat. My feet were sore, my neck was tight, fingernails still dirty from the vines. I shot up and burst through the archway door, trying to erase his eyesight, jogging through the hills, between nature's tendons and orbs, thinking about them, the glaciers, but also the light azure color, they were like Kajsa's. I needed to melt hers, and to do that, I had to stay here, lost in this little village, surrounded by its nature, not my memory's. The path of the run finished, disappearing into the woods, where I ran, further inland, harped by the sound of a brook, and dead leaves, her face forming glaciers floating away with the forest's darkness. When I let people die I pictured them in the ocean, treading water, because it was painful to remember death retrospectively.

It was a cool look, returning home in sweat.

«*Coucou!*» Marie chirped. Though she was the proprietor, at that point she and I had developed a kind deal, one where I contributed, filing paperwork, some accounting, whatever administrative tasks I could handle off the books. She liked my handwriting, the way my ts sometimes curved, depending on the preceding letter. She called it «type conscious,» and told me I'd be a *très* good monk, transcribing texts with precision and style.

She smiled from the balcony. Lunch.

I headed to the garden table. I didn't think to change, but realised this was a proper Sunday lunch. A red wine just uncorked, roasted duck, two lait cru cheeses, 6 o'clock baguettes — the warm, crisp kind.

Next to where I would be sitting was someone I didn't know. This is when I realized my XL t-shirt was not appropriate; I wasn't among family. My eyes could not turn, nay they wouldn't. I was afraid I was going to get used to this type of meal a lot, one where I had to be polite, to curb what I was thinking.

I ran inside to take off my shirt, passing the kitchen. Marie was by herself, mixing a bit of frisée for a salad. The afternoon window light grazed the room, softening her apron from beige to cream, and the lettuce, a green now paler from the sun. I could see her arranging the frisée over and over, leaves elongating against the bowl, like thin long arms of sunbathers against the backs of beach chairs. As she moved her hands, their arms kept flickering between colours, pearl, pear, emerald, seafoam.

«Oh, hi Jeppe. Didn't see you.»

«Sorry to bother you,» I said. «Looks good.»

«Oh don't be silly. While you're here could you lend a hand?»

«Yeah sure,» I said.

Marie handed me some mustard.

«You know how to make a vinaigrette, yes?»

«Uh…»

Marie laughed, putting a hand on my arm.

«Yes, typical,» she said. «I will show you.»

It was quite simple in fact, adding the sunflower oil, and

lemon, though she said it was best to use olive oil, but with a big party, sometimes she cut corners, the good stuff being more expensive, and by the second glass, no one noticed anyway.

«See, all set,» she said. «Simple. Now go get dressed.»

Marie was, despite her strict accounting practices, particularly the way she double checked all the orders I filed, very kind. She was a friend.

A friend — a new friend — was a special type of category to elaborate upon. Similar to a sibling after childhood. Maybe it was arrogant for me to be the one to define it, but there were many types of relationships that we chose not to develop out of societal expectation and pressure. There was no rule that we had to follow conventions. Pressure demanded that we quickly fall in line, but again, I liked challenges. Most mornings I'd raise my hand and ask the attendant why couldn't I hang out with my friend after she was married… like why was everyone so against that? Most people here were heartbroken over the wrong type of love. Who said, anyways, we suffered from only one kind of relationship?

I walked through the kitchen's back door towards the little house. I was still living alone. Marie said no other workers were arriving, there was no need to find a place. Consider it lucky, she said.

I ran upstairs and tossed my t-shirt onto the floor. I changed into a nice dress shirt, splashed my face with a bit of soap and water, spritzing some cologne for good measure. When I returned to the table, everyone seemed to be a drink in. I thought to catch up but realized that rushing would look foolish. I eased my way in, slicing the duck and serving everyone, taking a sip as I went, still unsure if I should've made conversation with the guest next to me. That man in Sainte-Croix I tried to chat with, he refused to make light company. I didn't need the rejection of another stranger, or worse, him politing me, spritzing tiny lunch chat. I was a slice of duck away from feeling comfortable here, in the world of the vines, and he was my test. My new test. To fail the chat was to fail my chance to make a new life. But at the end of the meal, after chouquettes, the cream puffs, we looked at each other. He was calm. Like the rare moment of winter sunlight, warm just surrounded by such presence.

If he was only her. A Sunday lunch, plus the protected moments of anticipation. Someone I knew for years, that wouldn't hurt me if I said something stupid in a public setting. I wanted, no I needed. I needed more than strangers and acquaintances, and I wasn't sure I was going to get that quickly enough.

11.

I stopped by the Jamaican place. I wanted to try the food again, to see if it still tasted the same, magical, or if it was just novelty. Cheap. If I could use a French word, to *goûter* it, sample a new life within one bite. And if I could work here, maybe I wouldn't be very noticeable. No detectives were to look there.

Maybe the U.S. wasn't all money and corruption, and immigrants were the ones who kept it honest.

And if Marie had immigrated, I wondered if she would've done the same thing, and sample the surroundings.

«Hello,» I said.

Ini was behind the counter.

«Mm,» she replied.

She swayed, regal, as if she were wearing ballet slippers. Stage left, heat lamps. I looked at the fried dumplings, they were the oil orbs I remembered, but I looked up at her menu, and the curry goat sizzling, as if I could see the yellow powder flecked across the room.

«Yes?»

«I…»

«What would you like?» she said.

«The curry goat, it's good?» I asked.

She grabbed her tongs, clapping them together. «Mm.»

«The curry goat... do you goû — ehm, do you rec—

She started to plate it with a blood purple cabbage, and handed it to me.

«Your name?» I asked.

«My name?»

I waited, my hands between my pockets, looking at the time. 11:58am.

«Ini,» she said.

«Ini... I'm Jeppe.»

«You enjoy now.»

She clapped the tongs together, and closed the refrigerator, where she kept the cabbage. The blood trickled out, amethyst against the light, the tiny Jamaican flags billowing, yellow black and green, not money green, but like the food, herb green. I didn't see any signs. I'd have to ask her if she was hiring. I wondered if she'd just laugh at me. Crazy I think about that now, since my doctor laughs at me. If she can laugh at me, anyone could.

12.

We're not allowed to wear cologne. It's one of the only rules I don't like here, something about we'd drink it, but it's a shame. One of the things I liked most about the vineyard was the scent, the mix of smashed grape skins and broiling sugar in the sun.

I was lucky to get the grapes job and one day I might be so lucky to work at Ini's, to get that perfume in my system. I'd write about the place, just like I do at the hospital. Slip in that way, yeah, favor my own apprenticeships. From songwriter to journalist. Lucious, spicy, bright, herby. I could see the Boston Globe review already. The title: Scintillating.

The review would go like this:

A SIMPLE KIND OF FANTASY
special Globe Correspondent Jeppe

Driving into the parking lot, I could barely make it to the front porch without being blown over by the air of succulence. The fried dumplings, those orbs like baseballs bursting with oil from its seams. Oh, and the thyme.
But I found it odd — a business at the edge of a town at the edge of a state. The food deserved to be spotlighted, not competing with the fake scents at a laundry service. Shoreline

was beautiful, hypnotic, yes locals were nice, encouraging me to go on a dune walk, or see the breakwater, though I must confess that I did not want to leave this shop. There were trancelike qualities to good food, for it to be the center of the environment, even in a town like Provincetown, where nature was its premium. Could this shop not also be its premium?

I think that was one of Kajsa's points, now that I'm thinking of it. Not just enjoying the momentary flashes of time, but deciding to change our perception of time, based on what we ate, and where. It was hard for my cell mates to believe this.

I had no real friends yet, and Kajsa said when you didn't have friends, stop pondering about life, go get a real job. Stuck in this hospital it is a bit difficult to find a job, and a restaurant wasn't a real job, she'd say. Get a job you don't love. If you love it, you'll get too attached, for the wrong reasons. So I started my search at a coffee shop, like an American should've, looking for an unlovable job.

I sat on a bench outside the shop.

«Hey, Brit boy!» Foska shouted. She halted her bike mid-street.

I sighed.

«Not British,» I said.

«Yep, but still weird. What're you doing?» It was the first time I noticed her hair, neither black nor brown, but maple syrupy.

«I got to work on my résumé.»

«Yeah, toss it.»

She grabbed my elbow.

«I'm good, I need the space.» I shook off her elbow.

«That wasn't a request. You're coming.»

«No, no… I shouldn't.»

«What,» she said. «You have other friends I don't know about?»

We biked over. I got a little less skeptical of Foska when I saw how nice her place was. I saw the little garden, a bench with whale pillows. I was shocked no one had stolen it. I definitely would've, but this was small town trust. Maybe that's why Marie got away with her work, because who would doubt her? It wasn't strange that Foska would invite me too, or that expensive decorations were kept outside. It was part of the environment and its open hearts.

Foska's cottage was inherited from her parents. They were dead now, but she had stayed, second generation townie, home schooled, except for high school, when her parents thought she needed a preparatory education.

«Aren't you happy I invited you?» she asked. We walked towards the living room, and as she did, she took off her jacket, revealing a sweatshirt. I never realized how many layers she wore.

«Thrilled,» I said.

Part of what I missed was a home. My own home, one that people were invited over to. But since I'd been traveling, I hadn't had the opportunity to make others comfortable. It was always me as guest and outsider.

We sat on the sofa, and I sighed.

«You're a little bitch, aren't you,» she said.

I got up to look around.

In a glass cabinet I noticed all the syrup bottles. I had no supply of pantry items like that. At first I wondered if she was from a family of syrup producers. I didn't collect bottles, I wasn't from a family that worked the farm. In fact I had no sense of what a farm, or a vineyard was really like, until Marie had cultured up my life.

«And you're a bigger bitch,» I said.

One of my strange theories was about who we became attracted to, and who revolted us. Maybe our affinity was environmental, physical features reflecting the condiments we ate and worked with. Marie, that amber glisten, from the sweet grapes. Kajsa, from her summers of watercolor fog and horses. I was born by water, so of course I liked it. Syrup, perhaps, an indication of farm life. I was no barn animal.

«You were making coffee?» I said.

«Yah,» she said. She stood in front of the stove, boiling sludge granules.

«I learned this on a tour, downtown Boston,» Foska said. «A thick sweet coffhee, hee.»

Tours, one way we let outsiders become more familiar. They weren't the most intimate introductions to a city, but at least they were a start.

«I drink this?» I said.

«Now or never, Jacob.»

«Jeppe.»

I winced. It was sludge.

«Jeppe, Jakob, Jop. It's like duck duck goose with your name!»

«Someone spelled it Yep, if you believe it.»

«I'd like that person. Do I know him?»

«Her,» I said. «I doubt it.»

«Right.»

«What about my résumé?»

«Don't… just let it happen. Relax, okay? Relax. Do people tell you to relax? Like, stop by a shop, without a résumé. Smile.»

I scowled.

«Say hello. Say good morning. Ask them how they're days go, how they will go, ask very specific questions.»

I was afraid of specific questions. One of the luxuries of being an outsider was never having to ask the difficult, more intimate questions, the ones that led to rejection. We talk in therapy all the time about «guest to insider,» «GTI,» the only way to feel at home is to let go of the home we started with. It seemed counterintuitive to me, but I was tired of being the guest.

«Right…»

«And don't expect a résumé to do the work for you.» Foska was so forward.

«You got to be alive. Not dead, like, you just got off a redeye from Europe.»

There was no asking me to notice something about the day, or the hour, or the day within the hour. There was no subtlety to time, and I honestly couldn't tell if it was a good thing. I was giving up something sophisticated for a kook. Two kooks in a kitchen, you know what they say.

13.

Along Main Street I skipped, résumés in hand, bull eyes blazing, ready. Had to be alive, Foska said. I stared at the sky. The clouds here were puffy, light, dreamy. The 252 foot Pilgrim monument shot up in the background, and that too was a marvel. There was a watchguard up top. He held a blade, I think. A weapon of some sort. I couldn't prove it, but I swore the police were following me from the beginning.

I sneaked into a little café, hoping to escape the attention. I turned, and the lobby was twenty square feet, if that, a little landing pad with a host stand. To the left was a room with six or seven tables, a bar, a jukebox. Plus the long staircase. In the middle of the lobby, it shot upwards towards the second floor. I know what Kajsa said but maybe a restaurant job wasn't such a bad idea.

«Be right there!» a woman shouted. She trotted down the long staircase, the metal planks clanking as she took each step. She took off her apron.

«For one?» she asked.

«No, actually,» I said. «I'm uh… I'm here to see if there are any positions available.» I expected Marie, with a shovel, dirty, offering me a job on the spot.

«Work?» she said. She looked at me as if I were a child, foolish. It didn't help that I didn't know what I was doing, but her seriousness had comforted me. She had many freckles, and forest eyes, the cool blue of the sky that danced in and out of black trees at dusk.

«Yes, I could help serve, or maybe take reservations...» I didn't know if she expected me to talk.

«Come with me,» she said. She put on her apron and took me by the hand up the stairs. They were quite narrow, they could barely fit me and her.

At the top of the stairs, I saw the kitchen. Two chefs cooking and plating. One had grilled a piece of fish, whole, studded with green herbs. The other placed a half cup of rice on the plate, swirling some red vinegar bottle with the label «xo.»

«This,» she said, «is your job. Can you go up and down these?»

«Why... yes,» I said.

«All day?»

«What do you mean, all day?»

«You'd be running plates. I can't do that. I need to host and cook.»

Her logic made no sense to me, one because I didn't understand how restaurants worked, but also because I didn't see how she could be both up and down the stairs for both jobs.

«Sure,» I said.

«I can't pay you that much,» she said. She took off her apron again, this time laying it against the staircase.

It seemed wonderful, a place to work, with exercise, with good food.

Sometimes I walk around the hospital ward, with a kettle bell, looking like I'm about to exercise. Some of my other mates join in. It's a nice procession of energy, a way to foam up some community. Not real exercise though, not like the restaurant. Some pay, some stress, new flavors.

Good food, but it was a temporary solution. I didn't know if I could take the job. If it would end up like the vineyard, a quick fix, with long term damage.

quatorze.

Days passed in the fields, the beauty of a new partner. Today, it was the Frenchwoman Claudette. She smiled at me. She had squid ink hair.

«You look like James Blunt,» she said.

«The singer?» I said. I was clearing leaves from the vines.

«Ya, ya, but like from his music videos,» Claudette said. The way she picked away grapes, pruning the stems as close as possible, it was as if she was repairing something.

«The sexy videos,» she continued. I blushed.

«You're beautiful,» Claudette sang.

«I don't sing my lines,» I said.

«Cause I'll never be with yoo,»

«One whispers my lines,» I shot back.

I didn't think she was hitting on me but it was at least flirting. A way to create intimacy with people she wasn't going to sleep with — I was too young. Maybe it was her opportunity to keep celebrating the riskier frequencies of her heart, to reveal that our bodies and personalities were something to admire at all points of the day. It was a reflection I didn't enjoy.

«You're beautiful, it's true.»

«Shush!»

Marie zipped through the vines in her little truck, a go-cart of sorts.

«Please, quiet, quiet!»

«We were just chatting,» Claudette said.

«There is no such thing as chatting,» Marie said. She looked at our pails. «You are much too slow.»

«Yes *d'accord* we pick faster,» I said.

The boss restarted the little truck and zipped away, soil kicking up and into our lungs. I coughed.

«She's nice, eh?» Claudette said.

It was scary to answer a question like that. If I answered too politely, it could've taken a lot longer for her to have warmed to me. If I answered too honestly, I might've hardened impressions too quickly. It could've ruined the relationship right then and there. Flirtations vanished.

«Yeah,» I said.

«Piece of shit, old hag hardass.»

Claudette took her pail to the end of the vine, dumping it into the large bin of grapes. I stood there, watching her, and the rest of us, burned, bitten by wasps. From afar, in a car, or a bicycle, passing through, the vines look garlanded, banana sunflowers surrounding them. But in the interior, they took on their own landscape.

«Hey Claudette, c'mere.»

Claudette stood next to me, I think expecting a cigarette. She had this soft look, like she wasn't going to hurt me.

«Can't you picture a red piano, set in the middle of the field?»

«What?» she said.

«A light melody in concert with the buzzing of insects, and a harpist, atop the hill, composing something.»

«And what made you think of that?» she said.

«I don't know,» I said. «Make work beautiful, maybe? More pleasant?»

The others picking hadn't said anything, but it seemed like my comment was appreciated, not just with Claudette. Elias, for example, usually quiet, clipping leaves, that was his preferred music. But I saw the red t-shirt he had worn today. I think he liked the red piano idea. He glanced at me, the sunburnt eyes glistening. He dropped his pliers and stepped over to me, dribbling his fingers in the air as if he was playing.

Claudette held my face. «Right.»

I think she didn't want me to change. I was this odd little creature who thought of vine work as music. But I was changing, with a new decade of acquaintances.

15.

I had to decide if I should take the job. But to take the job was to choose how to live. Marie had said that. No, sorry. The hostess said a job that didn't pay well enough to save, that made you work seven days a week, was expected. If you asked for a day off she'd say you have a day off — nighttime — as if it were healthy to work seven days a week, and then, like a phantom choir, an employer would sing, «go, until we tell you to stop.»

There was a perverse relationship to work in tourist towns. You had to work later before the money dried up now. And — even if I took it, I had to get a second job, maybe a third to help pay the rent, to enjoy Provincetown.

In our theater improv class, I act it out to the others. «Don't stop, dare not ask for health insurance.» That's too serious an expense. The patients would nod. «Don't even bother coming in, go to the beach, to the breakwater, go somewhere else to enjoy life.» I never heard «enjoy life» from anyone working here, just those who already had their millions, or exploited the millionaires themselves, which seemed on some level a dangerous form of masochism. I thought Marie said people worked to live, not live to work.

«Alcohol and cigarettes work to blunt an idea of freedom, young man.» That was from high school, but still, I saw a lot of drugs in town. People coped with live to work, *non* I could not accept that idea, I refused to live to work I was going to work to live even if I couldn't figure out the best way to say no to her, *oui* there had to be a good excuse otherwise it's a small town and she'd see me around and be like why didn't you take the job and I couldn't say what was within!

«Jakob, Jakob,» Foska said. «Calm thyself.»

I was at her place again, for another coffee. I liked hopping by, it gave me someone to talk to. I liked my own apartment, but you could not make friends in isolation.

«You want that job?» she asked.

«No,» I said.

«Then don't take it,» she said.

«But I need the money,» I said. «Or I can't afford health insurance, or my rent.»

«Please,» Foska said. She laughed, popping back another espresso. «You're gonna solve all our problems in one swoop? Let's start small. I need a new friend.»

«Hey, you're trivializing me.»

«I'm kidding,» she said. «Take a joke. I like you, Jeppoo.»

«Look,» she continued. «This town used to be a place for dreamers, for artists. I would know, I'm a painter.»

She got up, and turned off all the lights. She grabbed a flashlight.

«Instead my pretty, it's a resort ort ort ort.» She started to cackle, like a witch.

«Isn't that a little simplified? I've seen people here on a good time.»

«No time frame except money! Wine bottles with extra

sugar!»

«What'd you say?»

«Sort ort ort ort ort ort.» She cackled again.

«No, after that. Sugar.» I said.

«Oh, wine bottles with extra sugar.»

«How'd you know that?» I said.

«What, you don't know about that trick? Everyone knows about that trick.»

«Well I don't.»

«That's 'cause you live in a jukebox. No offense to your music dreams.»

«Why can't we reclaim it?»

«You just can't stop momentum,» Foska said.

«Yes you can. You could paint.»

«No, I said I was a painter. Past tense, Mr. Yep.»

«You could start a gallery —

«You can't just stop momentum.»

That wasn't true, I thought. It just wasn't true we couldn't stop our fates.

«Gotta go, Fosk.»

It didn't seem like she cared about paint or maple syrup, that is to say, the value of artists.

«Wait, what?» Foska asked. «You just got here.»

«Something I gotta take care of at the apartment.»

I was learning to lie. To lie on a much deeper level, was a skill. But Foska, and people like her, people new, I had to be careful with why I lied. She was someone I had an opportunity to be honest with, for there was no history. I'm not saying I've never lied before, or that history forces you to lie, but there was some thrill to now being conscious of it. It was fun. I could tally my lies, it was a new art of my game.

«Alright Jeppie,» she said. «Stop by whenever.»

I collected my helmet and jacket, heading out the door.

«I'll be here!» Foska said.

I biked to Ini's place. I was ready to finally ask her.

I got to the place, and just stood outside, thinking about what I'd say. I inhaled the salt air, the scallop shells, the blue plum sky. If work could not provide joy or health insurance, there was always new art.

I thought I'd prepare a speech, look official.

«Hey Ini,» I said.

I walked up to the display, waving, but not smiling, nothing *très* too friendly.

«Mm,» she said. «Yes hello.»

«Hello, yes.»

She took me in a bit longer, her eyes fixing on my t-shirt. I had worn the same one as last time. «The goat again?»

«Y— no, actually. I was wondering if you needed help.»

«Hm?»

«W- with the shop. Maybe the paint can be re—

«No, no, I'm fine now. Countin' m' thanks.»

«Oh…» «No, I am a painter. Well, a musician, but I am quite good with colo—

«I said fine now. Thank you.»

I wondered about Ini. How she got here. Maybe she wasn't from Jamaica.

«You live here?» I asked.

She looked up, but did not smile.

«Local.»

«No, but the Caribbean,» I said.

«From the United States,» she said.

«What?»

«You're from the United States,» she repeated. «If you say I'm from the Caribbean.»

«I grew up here, in New England,» I said.

«Then I'm from Jamaica,» she said.

Seasonal migration, like me in France. Laborers that traveled, except it wasn't wine that bound us. There was something more American here.

«I...»

She started to put away some dumplings.

«You enjoy now,» she said.

Like last time, I bought some of the goat, before heading over to Foska's.

A police car rode up beside me.

«Nice haul,» he said.

«What?» I asked. I thought he was pointing at the scars on my hand.

«Got myself some too,» he said. He held up a plate of the goat.

«Oh, right!»

He knew. So that's when he'd tell the doctor I wasn't paranoid. The officer would explain that new food was new art.

I biked towards Foska's. I dismounted. I touched her front door handle, the color stained. My fingerprints were painted turmeric. The goat. Coagulated memories. What I ate was what I felt.

«Je je je,» Foska hurtled. Her chanting was getting a bit annoying, always interrupting my thoughts. The hospital lights flickered.

«Yep,» I said.

«Oh, Yeppe. Why so glum?»

«Nothing, nothing. Tough to find a job.» Ha, I was avoiding the police. It didn't bother her.

«Yep, that can wait.»

«Why don't you swim with me?» she asked.

«Now?» I said. I never swam, though the doctor said the best ideas were new.

But swim. Now. Time was only forward, linear without a hereditary clutch. I was afraid Foska was the holographic of a sibling. A mirage, someone who might seem like what I was searching for, but only because what surrounded me was desert. I had to resist what was just an illusion of family. Stop Jeppe, you're upsetting me.

For the first time again, I would trust a decade sister.

«Now. My cousins got a place.»

«I didn't know you had cousins.»

«Je je yeah. Duh. C'mon, let's go.»

We arrived at her cousin's house to a pool party.

Boys. It wasn't my style but I liked their bravado, splashing into the water, paying no attention to nobody except themselves, even after summer's insanity. Fall freedom, a season for locals.

They were relatives, Italian, I imagined from her mother's side. When they emigrated here, I'm not sure. There were two boys, a blonde with sun dimples, and an older lanky, heavy tattooed, dark haired and dark eyelidded, almost southern Russian, from one of the -stan countries.

We walked into her cousin's place, a two level house with a view of the ocean. Much cleaner than my apartment.

«Chips?» Foska offered. Potato chips, set in a light wooden bowl.

I grazed the bowl with my index finger.

«One of my dad's old buddies. He's a ceramicist.» The town had many artisans, Foska explained.

The chips slouched, drooping like wilted petals. It was an elegant flower arrangement informalized, edible. And Foska, edible too. She and the town were becoming sweeter, little doses of sugar and relief. To trust a sister was to trust a town. It could work out. Work could work out. I just had to be less serious, more playful.

Salt air danced through the windows. Scallops and razor clams steps away from the apartment, gasping for water. Life, with death.

seize.

The sun was setting, its glow set against barns and the silhouettes of horses. In the echoes of neighs, I stumbled upon the local bistrot. A poorly dressed man was entering the restaurant.

«A glass?» he said, clasping his hands together, praying towards the hostess.

«Right away, monsieur,» the hostess said. She covered her face to cough before exiting to the kitchen. She brought back a glass of sweet white.

He was wrapped in tweed, a medieval serf, his forearms caked with dirt and dried sweat, his mustache long and unkempt, like snapped spaghetti strands.

«Gianluca,» said the Italian.

«Jeppe,» I said. He didn't say anything back, «nice to meet you,» or even a grunt, something that would make me comfortable, like I wasn't alone. It bothered me that he wasn't smiling.

«And you're here for?» I said, restarting the conversation. But there was no reply.

His silence was odd. I was making a sincere attempt.

«Wine,» he said.

«You know the area then?» I said.

«No, no,» Gianluca said. «I do this type of work now. Before

I cooked polenta,» he said.

«Polenta?» I raised my eyebrows, and turned my body towards him.

«In London,» Gianluca said. «My specialty. I had four kinds.»

He was like many of the workers, wandering through the villages until a vineyard said yes. That was typical of work like this. Anonymous, with past dreams.

«An ex-polenta master,» I said.

He was someone formerly defined by his profession. A dentist, a stock trader, a chef. That was a common way we introduced ourselves to each other. Now a grunt.

«Do you have a specialty?» he asked.

«Me? No. I'm a writer.»

«A poet? Do you seek inspiration?» He moved his hand towards the fields, pointing.

«No, I'm a songwriter,» I said.

«Let me hear it then,» he said.

«I don't sing,» I said.

«Right, you're an artist who doesn't show his work,» he said, laughing. He lit a cigarette he had been rolling between his fingers.

«Me, you see, I was showing the world. Cheese, mushroom, meat ragù, and fried.» He was just rattling off his expertise. I didn't understand how he could be so at ease. I thought I was taught to ration love.

«But you… you stopped,» I said.

Gianluca held his glass closer. «It was hard work,» he said. «Life, by credit card.»

«Oh. I understand.»

«No, no,» Gianluca said. «It was difficult.»

«Oh. You couldn't pay for things.» His life seemed simple. While he was a cook, and that was a category, he wasn't defined by it. If you went up to him at a party and he introduced himself, he'd say «Hello I'm Ginaluca,» and then turn to his drink, talking about the flavor of the anise. It would never occur to him to say «what do you do?» even if that was my tendency.

«Show me your work,» he said.

Even if someone did ask him at a party why he was a cook, he would shrug and say «no that's not true, I pick grapes now.» He had no need to talk about his past or class.

Gianluca glanced towards me, and then reached out to touch my fingers.

«There's no blisters,» he said.

His hands were callused, but warm, sensitive, and for some reason didn't smell of ash or tobacco.

«I wear gloves,» I said.

He took a sip of wine. «That's not what I mean,» he said.

«I'm sorry?» I said. I thought he was still talking about London.

He breathed in a little, then spitting out the dusk air. «No cuts.»

«What?» I said. I didn't understand why he'd think I'd be offended. It felt intrusive. But then I realized he was alone here, and that he was just making conversation with some fellow traveler. He thought I was also anonymous, that I wanted to disappear. For a second I debated that, if I could vanish, if I could become ordinary, and that was itself the makeup of a good life.

«Your fingers, why they do not have cuts?» You murdered her.

«Jeppe!» I heard a shout from just over the hill. Marie was waving at me, first a gentle wave, then furiously, beckoning.

«Kajsa,» I said. His eyes were black. «She threw me against a telephone poll.»

«I see,» he said, nodding, his fingernails scraping against the wooden table, drawing scratchy swirls, clouds, clouds pulled from the sky closer towards us.

Kajsa was about to cross the street, and before she could a car had accelerated. I shoved her.

«Jeppe, Jeppe, it's time.» Marie had walked down the hill, in long, fast strides. She approached our table.

«Good day,» said the Italian.

«Good day,» Marie said. «Good night, actually. Sorry to interrupt but I must at once speak with Jeppe.»

«Please,» he said, waving me away, like sheep cattle, or a child, something lesser. He continued to scratch the table.

«Kajsa!» I shouted, echoing at her in the hallway.

«Good… good day.» But the Italian had turned his body away, lost in some private thought. Marie could not stop talking as we walked back up the hill.

«And this is where it's most important, Jeppe,» she said. She started counting on her fingers, one, two, three, two fingers, then four fingers, her whole hand, then her thumbs linking, wiggling ten fingers like dollars, or probably millions of dollars, knowing her. I didn't know why she seemed so urgent though. We did most of the accounting on Mondays. «I need you to see this as very important. I need you tonight to do me a favor.»

«A favor?» I asked. We walked along the cemetery next to her château, the headstones curved, like ears, listening. Kajsa's limbs, lingering. For the first time I noticed how much Marie was limping.

«Yes, a big favor, in fact,» she said. «Please, with me.» She put her hand against my back, motioning for me to follow her to the interior of the cemetery. I loved being let in on her secret, well, what seemed like a secret. We stopped next to a tree.

Marie bent over to rub her leg, and then with her hands began to dig up a crop of soil.

I was surprised I was here, so close to her and also the Earth, it felt more personal than just accounting business. The cemetery puzzle.

«What're you doing?» I said.

Marie yanked out two little vials, which looked like tinctures, golden, like the wine she produced, but still, there was something off.

«It's tradition,» she said. «Tradition that you bury a little bit of your best harvests, on the first day of November.» I think she was talking about a Samhain of sorts, supposedly the end of the harvest, but we continued to pick late in the season here. It felt intimate that she was explaining this to me, the knowledge felt specific, like only an insider would know. Yes, if you were part of the sweet wine business, you were special, free from mechanical harvest most vines had now trucked. You were human. I was human. I wondered if this meant I was meant to be here, in France.

«I am burying the vintage from the year previous, so even if there's a bad year, really it's always a good year, for we've buried the best.» I pictured my headstone. Here lies Jeppe, producer of the finest sweet white in the world.

Marie took this moment to tap her index finger against one of the vials, pressing her ear against it, like a doctor with her stethoscope, listening, but of course to me she looked like a mad rabbit, her breathing increasing, no longer the doctor but the patient, desperate, panicking.

«It's tradition, a tradition I started some time ago, before I had such big vintages. Such successful vintages, I should say. You know we're not Sauternes, but we still make good wine here. The taste, it matters. It matters to us, it matters that we've kept the rhythm of this place, even if we cannot dominate the industry, or be known for something big like physics discoveries, you know?»

«I still don't understand what you're asking of me,» I said. I tried to be polite, since I couldn't stomach being the sole inheritor of her business. At least not at this point.

Her eyes were glassy, as if prepared to weep. Perhaps it was just the moon, glimmering against her mostly black hair, the occasional white strand like thunder shocks. She reached out to caress my face.

«This isn't from a vintage,» she said, bowing her head forward, away from me. She clasped the vials together, clutching tiny birds, wrapping them ever so delicately as she staggered forwards, drunk, through the cemetery and up towards the collection of vines just outside her house. I followed her into her garage, where she took a spray bottle into her hands, loosening the lid. She stepped to the large utility sink, turning the faucet on, spraying a huge force of water into the bottle. She stopped the faucet, water dripping still in the sink, cold blinks, as she looked up to me, handing me one of the vials.

«Put a drop in,» she said. I loosened the top, an eyedropper of sorts, and let a dab of brass yellow descend into the water, a slow infusion of trumpet and trombone. She took the vial from me and held it in her hand, her index finger now touching the tip of it, like a gun.

«It's a synthetic flavoring,» she said. «Tastes like honey, apricot, what have you, but it isn't.»

«What?» I said, then scanning the garage, looking at the plaques, 2012 best vintage, 2013 best vintage, marks for «complexity,» «sophistication.»

«I need you tonight to put this in the vats,» she said. «I'm testing a new technique, and it is a lot of work, but with my leg getting worse these days I figured you could help me.»

«This is illegal,» I said.

She laughed, placing the two vials onto a shelf, then walking over towards me, a hand on my shoulder. «I'm sure we can make arrangements,» she said. «Something that cuts preoccupation. You Americans, always worried about the law, and being happy.»

«It is not a preoccupation,» I said. It wasn't legal, at least, it didn't seem right. I knew that in the U.S. laws were constantly argued, sometimes things were skipped over, I mean, I got away with what I did, but I thought it was wrong of France. Here everything felt the opposite. The way the shop owner said 'less expensive, just as delicious.' Good quality, always, over individual profit.

«The way you look some days,» Marie said. She held her hand

on my shoulder. «It's like you think I spoke to the police.»

«No.» I took her hand off my shoulder.

«Consider it not a thought then. It is your 'app-iness.»

«Why do you need to do this?» I asked. «I'm sure your wine is good, so so good without help.» She didn't react, so I thought if I joked about her accent, she'd find it funny, and let this thing go. «So good, *oui, très fantastique.*»

«Consider it a favor for me, something I guarantee will bring you satisfaction.» She then pointed to her awards. «Surely this is a vitae pleaser, yes?» She had joked with me sometimes, wondering if I had arrived for a résumé.

«No, no, you're joking,» I said.

«You can,» she said. She stepped right towards me, and placed a finger on my lips.

«This is wrong!» I shouted.

I thought I knew Marie. But the relationships I was learning about were fractal, even if Foska had acted them forward.

«Wrong, wrong,» Marie said, sofly. «It rhymes with excitement, yes? We could say, fortune for your next days, because who knows when's the next time you'll get this opportunity?» She dripped a weak smile and grabbed the vial. She placed a new drop onto one of her fingers, pressing the liquid against my lips, smearing a gloss, a strong perfume of what to me was now full nausea, headache and feeling this moment as if someone from a nearby farm was going to walk in, or the Italian, yes the Italian, saving me, asking me more about my fingers, about the last time I pushed her someone away.

«He was a musician too, you know?»

Marie turned away.

«My son. I was too hard on him.»

She crouched down, and rested her leg. She placed the vial near the sink. She pressed her hands to her face. I didn't know what to say, but her son, it felt like he was a part of me. At the karaoke bar in Provincetown, the one I'd go to months later, I saw this guy performing and he had the same motion. During the sad part of the song he pressed his hands to his face, just like Marie. It's strange to think that these two moments were connected, but that's the only way I could justify why, of all people, I had met Marie. I believe that's part of growing up, hearing the failed stories, so that every time we hear someone in distress we can appreciate both the good and the bad without getting too involved.

«Was he talented?»

«He was very good.» Marie smiled, eyes glassy. «He never had a chance.»

«No,» she continued.

She grabbed a vial. I think she was forcing me to do something. Instead of a crazy artist dream, or some one in a million chance — one in four million, according to the real odds of making it as a songwriter — she was saying, no, this is not the right pursuit. No, I'm sorry.

She, unlike Kajsa, was trying to steer me towards a more stable career, a more stable path. I'm sorry, you're not doing the right thing. Vials, her symbol, her child. A way to avoid the hospital. Seventy percent of the people here were artists.

«He suffocated from love.»

«Oh.»

I tried to step towards her, but she turned away.

«I'm sorry.»

«You don't have to help me,» she said. «He would've done the same thing as you.»

She sat in darkness, against a barrel, its skin puddled red. Marie doodled on it, a couple of zigzags with her finger, scratching more and more, composing a simple, sombre melody.

There wasn't much I thought I could say, or do, except watch her. I held her wrist, and tended to the pain. For that moment I was sane.

17.

We have one t.v. here, in the cafeteria. It's so some of us have something to look at, in case we don't want to talk to each other at the very time we're all expected to have conversation.

When Foska turned on the television, she knew, maybe, that tennis was a logical thing to introduce me to. She knew I'd be a good coach, or play-by-play announcer. Tennis wasn't a contact sport. I didn't have to share things directly.

I loved thinking about all the variety of options. Even now I keep a notebook under my bed frame. We have to prove we were working towards something once we were out of here. I told the doctor I was studying for my teaching certification. Think she was impressed by my level of detail.

slice a shot used to mix up the pace or velocity. In French, *le slice.*

le slice used with a continental grip, and with the proper closed stance footwork, stepping into the direction of the ball or slightly across your body. You had to take the racquet back with not just your arm, in fact it's your entire body. *bodee* (French accent).

bodee your non-dominant hand — my left — remains on the throat of the racquet. You can think of it like you're choking someone, but just as you're about to choke them, it's a light grasp. Contact is almost parallel to the net. When you move into the shot, your non-dominant hand releases back, for counter-balance, floating, almost like a ballet move. A good slice can also be turned into an *amorti*, or drop shot.

amorti in French, drop shot. Nothing to do with *mort*, dead.

There was so much to learn about tennis. And great too, it was a sport that didn't offer as much prize money as football, that wasn't about money at all. The t.v. announcer spoke of it as a lichen, something that grew like joy, over and upwards all forms of roots and ages.

«Chips?» Foska said. I held a couple. Gold petals.

The match continued and we sat, sort of quiet. I kept a little notepad, writing fragments here and there.

etiquette gossip rumblings, crowds do not appear to yell as in other sports. quiet is the decorum.

It was time to leave, the match not over but I would finish my play-by-play at home.

«Do you like my cousins?» Foska asked.

«Why... yes,» I said.

I was a bit taken by the question.

«I like them too,» she said. «Sometimes too annoying.» She smiled, and then sunk into the couch. A cracked leather, ripped-up sofa, like a frayed teddy bear, its left eye popping out.

«They can be a — They're lonely.»

She picked at the sofa's stitching. I looked at her.

«They're not lonely,» I said.

«Uh huh, well,» she started. She muted the t.v. I saw Kajsa. We were outside my apartment.

She knew not one thing about what it was like to be lonely.

«Notice it next time, their voices. My family's everywhere.»

«Everywhere...»

That was a strange concept, saying that you were lonely because you had too much family.

«Yeah,» Foska said. «Check the cemetery. Littered with my family, it's gross.»

18.

I spent the next morning roaming the cemetery. I was looking for Foska's family to see how many of them were buried here. Weeds and skeletons. The occasional crow, perched atop a piece of marble. It groaned towards the sky, the color of blue plum.

I thought if I saw their plot, gravestones of all shapes, family members of all ages, I'd realize she knew what my definition of family was. An uncle next to a nephew, a niece, a cousin, a mother, a father. That'd be more family than I ever knew.

I preferred the graves in the meadow, *en plein air*, a hundred feet away from the rest. There were two tombstones, Lily and Marcus, ages twenty two and twenty four. It didn't say whether they were married, if they were even related at all. That'd be cool, I thought, burying yourself next to an anonymous companion.

There were more graves, probably thousands, but Foska didn't have that much family, I don't think. Besides, it was too depressing, thinking about all these deaths right now. I wondered how many of my friends here partook in accidents. We didn't talk about it per sé, but I could tell some had buried the truth.

I biked over to Ini's. I have to be honest and say that I wasn't jealous of Foska, it's just that the boutique was completely different, and that difference, like immigrants, was a major key to the survival of an ever-lasting population. There was a vibrant energy to the Caribbean somehow preserved within, and by the colors, something not American, something not French, something definitely not like these ghastly white walls, and I couldn't figure out why. Maybe it was because it didn't reek of money. Or that, truthfully, I doubt the police suspected a killer cooking jerk chicken.

Ini had a different relationship to the Cape, and that the colors and scents within her food must've formed that difference. Maybe it was crazy, maybe I was crazy, but I thought the different salt and spice content must've affected how my mouth moved, and creased. I was tired of chewing one way, and that wasn't a metaphor. If I were frying dumplings from the very beginning, no way I'd have been this messed up.

It helped I needed a job, too, because in America, that's how I was defined.

«Hey Ini,» I said.

I walked up to the glass display, where I noticed for the first time, no oil orbs.

«No dumplings?» I said.

«Mm,» she said. «They're fryin' in the back.»

«Oh,» I said. «The goat then.»

She clapped her tongs and the plate was mine.

«Here,» she said. She offered me a dumpling.

«Oh, delicious!»

«Ten dollars,» she said.

I offered her a ten.

«The dumpling's fifty cents,» she said.

«What?»

«That would be $10.50. Townie special.»

«Oh.» I realized she had gifted me the dumpling.

«Mm,» she said. «Yes?»

I was loitering.

«Oh, yeah. Yeah… you're. Well, the outside.»

«What about it?» she said, shutting off a heat lamp.

«Well the outside. It. I noticed. Well, it could be painted. Re-painted. No I'm not saying it's a little off or anything. Just I got a friend willing to paint it.» I was involving Foska but thought of buckets. «She's got three buckets. I got three buckets of the exact colors outside.»

«Buckets,» she said.

«Green, yellow, and black. Yellow, green, black. Or… black — yellow — green.»

Ini walked back to the kitchen and grabbed a couple of dumplings, putting them in the display. She turned a heat lamp back on.

«No thank you,» she said.

I looked at the menu above. The ackee dimmed.

«Cool, cool,» I said.

«Mm.»

I walked towards the front door, ready to say «maybe next time—

«Enjoy your day now.»

19.

I dashed to Foska's, ready to upsell her new painting job.

«Foska, Foska!» I said. I knocked on her door.

It was a big thing to lie but I felt like I needed to prove myself. I couldn't stay in P-town if I had no purpose, no job. Foska was slowly becoming a reason I liked the place, and that was as good a reason as any to give myself a chance at a new life.

A minute passed, and no one had answered. I started to count the clock from 11:57, seconds of anticipation I enjoyed, that were now natural to me. 11:57:01, 11:57:02, 11:57:03.

The door opened.

«Hi,» Luca said. Foska's cousin, the older one.

«H— hi. Was looking for Foska.»

Luca opened the door a bit further. He waved me in, his index finger tilting, conductorbatonlike.

I waited in the entry corridor.

«Would you like an espresso?» he said. His beard looked thicker, his eyes, a green, darkened, burnt olive. He dropped a badge or something on the counter.

«Y—yes. Why not.»

His limbs reached out to the stove, leafy vines, forearm veins bluing as he ignited the burner. He resembled a treant, long stalks of branches ambling around the kitchen.

«Jeppe, right?»

«Yeah.»

«Welcome to Provincetown,» he said.

He offered me a little cup, espresso still frothing around the surface. He then staggered upstairs to Foska's studio space. He closed the door.

While I stood in the kitchen, the surviving foam bubbling into liquid, I noticed Foska's cabinet. She kept old porcelain tea cups. There was one that had a painted scene on it. Even though it was partly faded, I could tell from the background it was Massachusetts, the pale ocean.

I began to imagine more of the scene, driving up past the mill towns, university apartments, morning traffic, arriving into water towns, sea gulls, voiceless beaches. It was a trip along the I-95N highway and outer roads that was color specific to the off season, where everyone became part of that local economy, the mussels oysters clams and lobsters, the salt water the boiling broth for us all, except it was quite cold, the broth was freezing, the only thing that could warm me were the air of horses and dogs, and memories. The teacup, a portal to older sisters.

«Oh Fiona, come on,» Kajsa said. Fiona, a strong horse, trotted a little towards me, bowing her head, nudging me to scratch her nose.

«This is Björn,» Kajsa continued. Björn jumped right in front of Fiona, exploiting her skittishness. He bowed his head immediately, moving only when I walked away.

We stood for a bit in front of the woods. The forests expanded into thick pastures beyond. It was a bit difficult to believe this was the edge of the Boston shoreline, or at least a place I had forgotten, or failed to explore. That was the strange aspect of returning home. I thought I liked nostalgia, but new feelings clashed with old patterns.

I pretended we were sipping cider, and that our circumstances were different. Our fate could've been a rural life, training horses, cutting wood, selling off our extra produce to restaurants. And then I imagined it was the seventeenth century. Ale was our only option to survive the next couple of months, not as luxury but as necessity. Quickly that thought was discarded, I turned to other ideas, we were elves, awaiting the years after human wars, cloaked in our azure robes, scepters adorned with sapphires, cold lights of power.

«And last but not least, this is Dinii!» Kajsa chanted. Out of the house sprinted a sprightly dog, a German Shepherd pure bred. He almost looked like a fox, quick to scuttle between logs. I offered him a branch. He sunk his teeth in it.

Dinii took his time to show us the rest of the property. The furry creature wandered way up the hill, past the thin slit of land between two forests, towards the house on the other side. There rested Kajsa's grandfather, a civil engineer for the Massachusetts government. He immigrated here from Sweden. I never thought about Kajsa this way, linked to elsewhere, a forgetful effect of Americanization.

Dinii scratched his paw against the front door, waiting a moment, but hearing nothing he continued to the garden adjacent. There was a little gravestone, Kajsa's younger brother Marcus, who died, drowning.

Kajsa held me against her body, strands of hay stuck to her jacket. I felt them but not as hindrances. She picked one of them off, threading it through my hair.

«Hey Jepperie,» she said. A nickname, like reverie.

Dinii was still far above us. He caught a glimpse of a book laying against a tree. He rolled it over. It was Kajsa's diary.

Neither me nor the dog had read it, but in it was the worst of insults, doubts, confusions. Never to be a trainer, an architect, a writer, a teacher, a horticulturist, an anything. She was imprisoned to this land. It didn't make sense in a contemporary context, but maybe now I realized how little I understood of Kajsa. She was a New Englander, but Swedish by ancestry. A history of long dark winters and high rates of alcoholism. From communal villages to private agriculture. She couldn't forget that, I don't think, her history, which taught her cold dark truths, but I thought about the location she was in. In America, but elsewhere by oral and genetic history. It impacted what she saw, what she heard, what she tasted, how she felt. She, free from farm labor, but no longer full of possibilities. How could she, when the U.S. burned with debt and tempers.

The hay that Kajsa had threaded through my hair had drifted to the dirt below us. As Dinii kicked the diary around, Kajsa too was moving, snapping the strand with her boot.

«Hey,» I said. And that's all I could get out before I lost her. The souvenir was fading.

I was darting back to Provincetown, two hours south, where all the North Shore boats and beaches would be distant, Kajsa outside, surrounded by the horses. Without noticing, Dinii had escaped the white fences surrounding both properties, Kajsa's diary between his teeth. He had run towards the sea, dragging his nose through the sand, sneezing, whimpering a bit when a horseshoe crab nicked him with their pincers. He kept whimpering, glassy eyed, his fur ruffled by the winter breeze, the tide slowly bringing him and her away from shore.

20.

«Just let yourself in, huh?» Foska said.

My espresso was cold. I must've stood here for an hour, lost in teacup.

Sometimes I zone out from the medication, and I wonder if that's the same type of lost. That I'm supposed to forget where I am or who I was, as part of recovery, but I think there's a similar beauty in reveries. Can't tell whether you've suspended yourself in something more memorable than the unlinked movements of everyday life.

«N-no,» I said. «No, Luca let me in.»

«Ah, cool. I was at yoga.»

«Yeah, rad,» I said. I never said rad.

«You okay?» Foska asked.

I looked at the counter with Luca's badge.

«Oh yah,» I said. «Just the coffee. I forgot to drink it. And hey, I got us a job!»

«What job?»

«This Jamaican woman offered us a job. To paint her boutique.»

It felt so easy, life's problems resolved by lies.

«Oh, radd d d d d,» Foska said.

«You can paint it.»

«Me, no I don't paint stuff like that. But you, yes.»

«You could work on your brush skills.»

Foska hissed, and then snapped. «Do you know what Fine Art is?»

«The study of beauty by those in power,» I replied.

«What?»

It was too intellectual.

«The study of what you consider beautiful.»

«Fine Art is what I do,» Foska stated. «Brush work —

Foska began to imitate a wall painter.

«Is what contractors do.»

«That's classist.»

«No, it's how the world works.»

«You could even get some meals for free. Big and delicious.»

«Oh fuck off,» she said.

I looked at her walls, the faded colors, the bright colors.

«What kind of painting do you do?»

Foska got up to grab a painting and handed it to me.

«Miniature. But it's not like you care. C'mon let's celebrate!»

«But we. But I haven't even done anything.»

«You fine with cocktails?»

«At 1 p.m.?»

«It's Saturday. Hey Luca!»

As she shouted, I slipped the painting in my backpack. Foska threw a stone at the ceiling.

From upstairs I could hear the studio. A grumble was felt beneath the floor.

«What?» Luca said.

«We're making a drink,» Foska said. «Jeppe got a job!»

I heard no sound.

 «Something French.»

The door opened, a howl ajar.

Luca trotted down the stairs, with nice cocktail glasses.

«Well, if we're making drinks,» he said, holding up a glass. He smiled but Foska had taken over.

«Now,» she said. «A French cocktail, right.»

«An aperitif,» I said.

«What?»

«In the sense of a drink, it doesn't translate to cocktail. Here it's mixed with hard liquor.»

«Well, right. But it's a drink after lunch.»

«Afternoon. Well it's 1pm.» 1:03pm. «It's a bit after one.»

«Are you usually this annoying?» she said.

«It's charming,» Luca said.

I looked at him. He understood. Or he could understand. There was more than one way to live.

«Fine,» Foska said. «Teach me oh wise one.»

«It marks the end of the day, the turn to the start of the evening.»

«How interesting,» Foska said. She lit a cigarette.

«How interesting,» Luca said.

«We could say this is the Saturday aperitif, since you didn't feel like painting today.»

«I did paint,» Foska said. «Yesterday.»

I looked at her.

«Well, I guess Foska needs this drink the most, huh?»

Foska looked at me, tapping her cigarette out the window.

A Kir Royale. It was a simple thing to make. Champagne, with a lick of crème de cassis, the dark sweet red liqueur. I liked to imagine this was me being French, or at least pretending I could still be in France, live television imported for adults. But in reality this was something more serious. Food and drink were two of the most complicated and elemental decisions of our lives, even with delightful things like cassis.

That was one of the most horrible aspects to understand about the United States, but we frequently chose not to admit it. Kajsa said we loved sweet things. When I was doing that accounting work for Marie, she had made some offhand comment. She said here we had the Coca-Cola palette, which meant our tongues were so used to sweet things that it was impossible to taste sour things, or bitter things, like coffee. Coffee needed milk, sugar to mask the bitter.

But it wasn't just coffee. If you looked at any ingredients label, it had sugar. Take the food they serve here. I ask the kitchen and the cooks shrug, they say it's packaged from somewhere else. So, sugar. So it wasn't just a metaphor, the reality was we ate and drank so many sweet things that we couldn't even tell when something was meant to be bitter. And because we had so many sweet things, it was killing us. When I was at the hostel, I had heard something like that from a t.v. announcer. I remember because he had donut sugar powder still stuck on his beard, and the backdrop was Cape Cod. Forty percent of our population was obese eighty percent of our population was overweight, heavy clouds, darkening the signals. Yet it wasn't our fault, it went on, it was the realities of our bodies with impossible blind spots. We couldn't sense other realities. Maybe Kajsa had taught me something, not just about time, but about our senses in general. Maybe siblings from other upbringings were the bitter truth we needed, but our current representatives didn't know how to be anything except sweetly optimistic and infantile. We were constantly lied to, because the alternative was gruesome. We were stuffed with preservatives, kaleidoscopic shards of food, information, media — nothing was whole, holistic, universal. There was no stabilizing force. There were not enough honest sisters.

Foska already had two bottles of sparkling wine in the fridge.

«You think I can't have fun?» Foska said.

As I turned to place it on the counter, three glass flutes appeared.

«I wanted to try too,» Luca said.

I couldn't tell if he was lying, or if I was lying to him, since I imagined he had tasted one before, and surely he couldn't've been as ignorant as Foska. I needed him to see this as a joyful, sweet, but barely sweet; a drink that relented to America without too much sugar.

The crème splashed with acid currant, the sparkling wine rotating colors of red white and little blue, the American flag, at least this time, the lapis veins from Luca's limbs just a glance outside the frame of the flute. He picked up the glass to taste it, and as Foska stepped away from the window, one forearm grazed my shoulder. His eyes, olive, were struck by the sun, lightning to translucent green sea glass.

«To Jeppe's first job here!»

Foska's other hand knocked over a glass.

«Fuck,» she said.

It shattered.

«Let me see,» Luca said.

«Get away from me,» she said.

She turned to the sink. She was bleeding, more than I could ever wish upon her. Red pooled from her foot and around the kitchen floor.

«Ah god damnit,» she said.

I stepped up to the sink. I thought this was it, to be compassionate.

«I said get away from me,» Foska said.

It was Foska, I thought. But it was Kajsa.

We were sitting in my apartment, I was resting against the couch.

I was dizzy, I remember.

«You made that yourself,» Kajsa said.

I rushed to the toilet, to vomit. It pooled, cassis blood everywhere.

«Four?» Kajsa asked.

vingt-et-un.

The sun had paused, bleeding merlot sky. The clouds drifted water down onto the roads, the ground pattered different notes, a tap, a drip, a splash. I felt those notes were me, ready to be composed into something about Marie's son. Me, her son.

The tractor engine started, and I tightened my rain jacket, no longer looking at the sky, but coughing. My lungs scuffed with black smoke, and overanalysis. From the tractor I surveyed the fields with its tiny châteaus near invisible, faraway dotlets of brick amongst the rows and rows of vines. It was supposed to be pretty, but I couldn't appreciate it.

I glanced towards Marie. Her hands gripped the wheel, carrying us and the pails of grapes downwards to new slopes, new senses, first wild mint, then charcoal. She had not, as I could tell, seem to be partaking in this experience. Maybe her leg was hurting too much, but I could taste the cider. Amidst morning fog and the chill bittering French apple trees autumn kept present. I wanted to offer Marie a bite of the apple, here, taste it, and then all of us, Elias, Claudette, the others, we would take another bite, hollowing the core but retaining the sweet thin skin in our teeth, not in search of lost time but in search of time's product. It was unsettling to be in several places, but somehow it rooted me. One memory looped the other.

Claudette was smoking a cigarette while she picked, trading puffs with Elias between rows, sticking her hands through the branches. Their hands met, fingers touching like a dance, feeling one another's palm, then middle fingers, I was hoping, a provocative fuck off to Marie. I ripped through leaves, yanking chunks off the vines, rotten grapes mixed with noble grapes, not caring about *aigre*, anger, prizes, tradition, labor. Elias saw how quickly I was marching through the vines, and met me at the end of a row. I thought he was about to hit me. He took off a glove and then touched my neck, massaging it. I looked up to his eyes, the sunburn no longer there, but still, his blue eyes searing, glimmering a sense of electric fear. I wondered if he knew, if they knew. He tousled my hair, and put back his glove.

The whiff of tobacco past faded with the apple trees, and flitted with the wild mint. One moment I was in the fields, breathing in and out like a butterfly's movement, rapid, gentle twitches of air and heartbeat, the next my lips tasting a fetid honey, a spoiled ochre.

The drip of liquid was not from the clouds, but from the trickling of trumpet and trombone. Last night after Marie had left I stared at the vats, vials in hand, banners unfurling towards me, a procession of drums and slow applause from a wine tasting competition. An orchestra of drummers, each tap of the drum skin sanguine, the audience, each hand clap a shot of blood. Then winter, snow, descending from above, white powder and plasma, mixing, diluting the color of the scene to a crimson rust.

It was night by the time I got off the tractor. The town was unlit, pure darkness, except the sky, like an autumn water globe, stars hovering. The insects buzzed. The vines, now just country shadows. I didn't want to go home, so I laid down on a bench, facing the bus station.

«Are you okay?» Marie asked.

From the distance I heard her. I turned my head and just like the first night, she held a shovel.

«Yes,» I said.

Marie stepped closer. I did not move from the bench.

«Yes, long day,» she said.

It seemed like she cared. No matter what was said before. I believe that was forgiving, thinking that she still trusted me.

«Do you think we'll get a day off soon?» I asked.

«Off?» she said. «This is harvest. We pick when we pick.»

«Right,» I said. I curled my legs up on the bench. «Fuck you then.»

«Child,» Marie said.

«Con artist.»

«Off,» she said. «Skip tomorrow, sure. See you Friday.» Marie dragged her shovel across the gravel, etching my initials, and then walking away, dragging her leg.

I think I was downgrading a new relationship, and it felt good. There was so much pressure, because there was responsibility, and expectation. New relationships were like dating, you were permitted not to care after a while, but you had to communicate that deathlike «it's over.» But of course I was a bit nervous. It's not like I wanted to be fired. That was truly irreversible.

«Off,» she said, muttering up the hill, laughing to herself. As she retreated towards her château, the shovel pattered against the ground, softening against the buzzing of the insects. I imagined what I would do on my day off and it occurred to me I still had a vial of Marie's in my pocket.

22.

«Did you make that yourself!» Kajsa texted.

I saw her message but didn't think it was real. She was returning while I was laying in bed, I could not tell the exact time. It was morning. I was sick from four cassis. I leaned over to my notebook, which had a sketch of some vines. I scribbled «Sainte-Croix-du-Mont, dusty vial.»

«Four?!!» Kajsa asked, with two exclamations.

«I lied,» I said. «To my friends here.»

«Ah I already knew you were a liar,» Kajsa said. «That's what makes you a good music man. Besides, you're more like a warrior, remember?»

I was at this point sipping coffee with her, by my bedside. She liked decá, decaf, or mocha, in a little purple glass cup. Like the little cups we got here, with milk and happy pills.

«So you're okay,» she said. I had texted her in the middle of the night, call me! I guess, I saw 00:00 on my phone, it reminded me of the way the French used military time, it reminded me of the vineyards, it reminded me of France, then time in general, Kajsa time, memories going further and further back until I could figure out when exactly she disappeared from influence.

I'd like to finish the story there with her, the end of the coffee. A quick goodbye that let her flow away, like the tides.

«No, I'll take the plates,» I said. «Let me clear.»

«Oh *merci*,» she said.

«*Je vous en prie, Mademoiselle*,» I said.

«Doesn't that slice sound nice when we speak French? Will you go with me one day?»

I winced, trying to remember that she was just a holographic. I tried, I really tried to stay within one memory, but small things kept me between past and present figments of my imagination. Little spoons, the bowl of sugar, the pills, a napkin, our two cups, a drop of coffee still on the rim. I licked hers. She laughed.

«Gross,» she said.

As she laughed I looked at the clock. 10:57. I wanted her to keep on going, answering the phone, shrieking out my lies. I looked at the clock again, 10:57:02, maybe? 10:57:something. Right then Kajsa was blurring. Foska must've still been sleeping, her alarm clock going off. I dropped the coffee cup. It shattered, flattening into a mosaic. Something I wanted to keep lying about, but could not, without seeing the blood, the cassis, it was on Foska's floor, surrounding me and Kajsa.

23.

By the afternoon, hangovers faded. Foska wanted to surf. She said it helped her sweat off the final drops of alcohol. I didn't know how she had all this energy. Kajsa was always tired after we drank. Foska, she just kept going.

«But I don't know how,» I said.

«Britboy, learn to shut up,» she said.

We got to the beach. No one was there, I was worried, but Foska kept telling me that this place was far out of everyone's way.

«Look, you need to learn how to surf,» she said. «It's a rite of passage.»

«A milestone?» I asked.

«What?» Foska replied.

«A milestone, like, this is it, I'm a local, I can surf.»

«No, a rite of passage,» Foska said. «Who gives a damn about milestones?»

Siblings were milestones. To choose the right person in your adult life and it was just like a marriage proposal. The same level of fear and excitement, would this person love me forever and ever? Yes, I do!

«Why isn't Luca here?» I asked.

I wondered why Foska hadn't invited Luca. There, an evening

ago, enjoying the cassis, and now, us alone. Was she jealous?

«What? Luca already knows how to surf.»

I picked up my phone to text Luca.

«What're you doing?» Foska asked.

«Inviting Luca,» I said.

«No.»

I started to call Luca.

«No, stop,» Foska said. She took my phone, and started to call him.

«What's the matter, jealous?»

«It's obvious what you did, Jeppe.»

«I didn't steal him from you,» I yelled.

«I'm talking about Ini, you idiot.»

«Huh?»

«Were you trying to put my artwork up? Some rumor swirling from one of my buddies who knows Ini.»

«I'm sorry.»

«You little devil.»

«No, I'm a djinni.»

«A what?»

«A djinni. From the Arabic, an intelligent spirit of lower rank than the angels, able to appear in human and animal forms and to possess humans.»

«Listen,» she continued. «He's not your type.»

«What?»

Luca appeared out of the corner of my eye, on the far end of the beach.

«He'll kill you.»

I started to laugh. «He can't kill me.»

«Oh so you admit it,» she said. He's not the first to die.

«I didn't say anything.»

«Don't help me again.»

«I won't tell you anything about my life, fine.»

«No.» She raised a finger to point at me. «Admit that you like him.»

Before we started I saw something in the distance, it looked lifeless. I knew something was wrong because Foska hadn't moved. She couldn't see the body.

«Oh come on,» she said. «You actually like me? What am I, a sister to you?»

«You're everything to me.» I was talking to Kajsa.

The tide flowed back in, towards the chalk blue of the ocean, foam, jetsam, twirling seaweed. Memories drifted. There was a police siren.

«Wait!» I shouted. Wait!»

«Right,» she said. She looked towards Luca, and started to talk to herself. «I'm just another girl in a townie's way.»

Foska picked up one of the conch shells rooted in the sand. She took a stone, and started to grind away the shell's pink edges. Talc powder like makeup flew off the shell. The dust that was left, she scattered the ashes.

«No, stop. You are like a sister,» I said. «Really.»

I said it as if she knew how hard it was to say something like that.

«Isn't this perfect!» she shouted. A couple feet in front of her a little boy picked up sea glass along the beach. Strange, no parent, no one holding his hand. Azure, crimson, lily white bottle fragments, and humid drips of red. A vial, too, with seaweed vines, strangling its neck. The boy skipped them into the ocean.

Above the boy a sea gull squawked. Its beak had a grin, and gawked at Foska.

«Ha, ha, ha hu ha hu ha.»

«Scary,» Foska said. «Ba zee za zah.» She zonzonned, inventing buzzing noises that would piss off the sea gull.

The boy was laughing now. «Za zf zs za,» he said, imitating Foska's squawks.

It wasn't even dinner time, and he had spent the brief sunlight glaze. I could barely recognise him. He looked sad, alone.

«God damnit I feel trapped here!» Foska shrieked.

I watched the body float in the water. It floated past the ocean chalk and shark tips, fins and whale sirens, farther up north, frozen ocean. Foska was getting too close to the truth, I thought, and so I had to just imagine those who died as bobbing objects. I had to push old bodies away, further and further into the ocean. This, I now realized, was how I erased away the pain of Kajsa. I'd tell the officer this.

The torso floated in the water. The boy waved at it. Foska smiled as if it were her only moment to frame the image. Officer Kaplan, this is how Jeppe did it!

She walked past two docks before deciding to hike the stairs up to Main Street. All this, the mismatched observations, the split screens between how she viewed things and how I viewed them, both our versions were true, since she wanted me to admit I was a murderer, whereas I'd dare to say I liked the embroidery of a memory, one where I've let people die through softer and softer flashbacks, stitched up by erosion, trading away as morning turned into night, and stars. There wasn't time for stars, unless the stars exploded. I had to let burn my brightest star, even if it was just a memory.

The sad truth was that I had to let Kajsa go. The doctor was right, I think. The only way to do that was to let her fade, for me to live my life forward, outside of normal time.

vingt-quatre.

My day off from the vines began at «Police.» That's all the royal blue letters said, not «Emergency» or «Police Station.» It was casual, as if rural force would've been hurt in reputation from glitz.

I stood outside the station. The parking spots had old dry white paint. An apple tree, and an advertisement for a wine tasting two kilometers down the road. One car.

I walked past a bike rack. Thirty wheels jammed up onto each other. It felt like the station was more a gymnastics center than a serious official building, but maybe that was the point. You shouldn't feel afraid to report a crime, because that's what I was about to do.

I fumbled with the vial in my pocket. My prints were on it, but surely that wouldn't matter. The police must've had sophisticated instruments, like on television, to separate contamination from reality.

«Your name?» the administrator asked. He did not look up from the computer in front of his face.

«My name?» I replied. Perhaps it was a bad idea.

«Yes, your name. For the system.»

«Jeppe,» I said.

«Sorry, please spell it.»

«J-e-»

«Jeppe, yes. We have it now.»

«I'm in your system?»

«Yes precisely.»

I was a bit confused. I know Marie had taken down all of our names, but I didn't think she was sending them anywhere. Maybe the agricultural union had it, as a legal requirement, and by default the police would too.

«And you are here for?» the administrator continued. His glasses were slipping from his nose.

«I'm reporting a crime.»

«Yes, that's understood.»

«I'm reporting a scandal.»

«A scandal or a crime?» he asked.

«Eh, I'm not sure. Does it matter?»

«Yes.» He hands hovered above the keyboard, ready to type my official statement.

«A crime,» I said.

I heard keys quickly move, like bullets.

«I believe a vineyard is using illegal production methods.»

The man adjusted his shirt collar.

«One moment.» He got up from his chair and proceeded to the back.

I waited in the lobby, looking up at the artwork on the wall. There was a photograph of three men, what I assumed was the unit. They held their caps in front of them, as if they were just starting to pose for a more official photo.

There was also a little coffee table, and some dusty books. One, «The Desert of Love,» with a bookmark. On it, someone had written a little note, what was now faint ink.

«We are, all of us, molded and re-molded by those who have loved us, and though that love may pass, we remain nonetheless their work.»

I closed the book, placing it back on the coffee table. I looked up again at the photograph.

«Jeppe,» a deep voice started.

«Yes, that's me.» I shot up. A police man with broad shoulders stood over me.

«With me, please.»

He led me through a corridor as we approached his office. He closed the door and motioned me to sit. A fan was buzzing.

«I'm Inspector General Mauriac. I have been in charge of this station for fifteen years now, and oversee investigations into our more serious cases. I'm sure my assistant at the front explained all this to you.»

«Yes,» I said. I started to sweat profusely. The fan was not pointed my way.

«Now please,» he continued. «Please explain this crime you speak of.»

He placed his hand on a pad of paper he had on his desk.

«Scandal,» I said.

«What?» he asked.

«It is a scandal, not a crime.»

He breathed in the direction of the fan, I believe trying to cool himself off. He was at least thirty pounds overweight. He coughed and then reached under his desk for a pack of cigarettes.

«Would you like a smoke?» he said. He lit himself one.

«No thank you,» I said.

He took a puff, and then exhaled.

«Now, remind me, I was told this was a vineyard scandal you said?»

«Yes. In the area.»

«And which vineyard is it you're reporting?»

He tapped the cigarette over his keyboard, which I realized was outdated at least five years.

«Château La Coste,» I said.

He kept the cigarette snug on the space bar.

«Ah yes, Marie's.»

«You know her?» I asked.

«Why yes,» he said. «We all know each other.» He smiled.

I tried to shift my seat to catch more of the fan, but it was of no use.

«Now tell me,» he continued. «What is it exactly she is accused of?»

«It is not an accusation,» I said. «It's the truth. She cheats her wine.»

For the next couple of minutes I was describing the scenes I was privy to, when Marie had showed me the vats and shook the bottles with the amber yellow, how we went to the cemetery and she picked up a plot of land to give thanks for all the hard work she had endured. The inspector general nodded, listening along, taking a note where he saw fit, but after a while I noticed he had stopped writing.

«And what is your proof?»

I held out the vial from my pocket, and dropped it next to his notepad. He held it in his hand, like a jewel, before tucking it away into his jacket. For a moment I thought he was beginning to prepare a detailed report, but he just sat there, hands clasped.

«Now Jeppe,» he started, before a cough interrupted him. «Excuse me.»

He got up from the table and coughed into his shoulder. He sat back down.

«Yes, now where was I. Jeppe, this is a position I've taken for fifteen years. I've heard similar accounts as yours — not the same château of course, but vineyards here and there, tampering with the bottles and such. I must say that this is a serious matter, and I cannot just proceed with an arrest like that.» He snapped his fingers. «But I can assure you I will look into this.»

«Thank you,» I said.

«But you do know, this means I will have to stop by.»

«Yes,» I said.

«I will have to ask her questions. She might suspect something.»

«Okay,» I said. «And why's that an issue?» At this point I was drenched in sweat.

«Well,» he said, before one last puff of his cigarette. He stubbed it out on a bottle cap. «It means she might begin to wonder why this is all happening. If... well, how I got my information.» He smiled.

I walked out of the office as fast as I could, thinking many things. One, when he said that they were friends, that they all knew each other, that this was for sure a set up. Or maybe that it wasn't other châteaus that were being reported, it was hers all along, but if he was here for fifteen years it wouldn't make a difference. Even in the best of scenarios, that he was honorable, and it wouldn't matter, because Marie wasn't, and she'd certainly make me pay. And for that I realized I could not go back to the vineyard, at least not today. I hurried towards a main road and got on the first bus I saw.

We tunneled away from a familiar ambiance, the lone boulangerie sign, the dusty château, a ledge of fossilized oyster shells. Into view were blond façades, firetruck bridges, the Miroir d'eau. I could catch the scene, not of the village, but of the city. I had arrived at one of Bordeaux's main plazas.

All had passed through: a skateboarder, a bicyclist with a tennis bag, an old couple holding hands, a new couple lounged across the grass, a bottle of red wine, an ice cream cone and a *créperie*, a scootériste. I realised with landscape shock, I was in Boston somehow, sister cities connected. The same size, trading power, at least at one point in its history, but now bigger — Boston was bigger, yes. It was part of the U.S., the empire, whereas Bordeaux, no, that was long ago history, Napoleon no longer. Maybe us too, but not yet.

Kids squealed in the background. Lovers screaming too. I wandered and saw Place de Quinconces suspended in a vortex as summerfall romance and carnival rides went on, people continuing to pass through the quai. The angel was suspended above, and for a second it looked like the Pilgrim Monument. Blink and you could see other cities, maybe an Istanbul skyline now looks like 1940s New York. We have to look at ourselves in multiple places, otherwise a righteous mind would assume our present conditions as eternal.

My phone was buzzing at that point. Marie was calling.

The thought of France was a pull no longer of vines, and slow seasons, but quick, dramatic energy. The environment wasn't stable, it was a warm September. A coffee on the main street, with pancakes and Vermont syrup.

I looked at my elbows, dirty still from the other day. I then looked down at my feet. I was still wearing my rainboots. No one seemed to mind, but I felt shy, a bit embarrassed, craving ice cream to sweeten my feelings. My phone buzzed again.

I took the tram to a neighborhood a bit far out from the city center, where no one seemed to think my dirty boot was a big deal. Perhaps I was *mâlin*, bracing for the rain after this strange summer weather. I entered an ice cream shop, no bigger than a corridor, a whiteboard scrawled in pink lettering, «vanilla, with bits of pastry.»

«That's it?» I said.

Marie texted me.

«Yes, one flavor,» the scoopériste said.

He had curved a soft scoop of milk white ice cream, striped and studded with *canelé* pastry. He then had handy his spray bottle of rum, labeled just «R,» spritzing first the statue on the counter, a head replica of a slave face, and then my cup, me, the mist of sugarcane. What I barely remember, of course, was binging on four pastries, and later that afternoon, glasses of the Réunion.

Marie kept calling.

«Yes, hello?» I said.

«Your day off!» she shouted. «Have you given it a thought!»

«Yes, I am quite enjoying it,» I said, the vanilla on my lips.

«Hey, young man, not your day I'm talking about!»

«What?» I said. The rum was strong, but it could've been Marie.

«Have you given the wine a thought! The vials!» I could hear her, she was in the back room of the special barrels she kept.

«Eeeh, uhn, eeh eeuh,» she continued, imitating French ambulance noises. «They're coming to get you.»

I held the phone closer to my ear. I could hear her fingers tapping against the barrels.

«I'm thinking,» I said.

«Good, think like the sirens! Lock up and sedate you if I hear no!

Enjoy! Tonight you can help me! Okay bye Jeppe!»

25.

It wasn't my fault that Kajsa died.

She... I loved myself. But I loved her, maybe too much.

I thought about this as I biked across town. It was becoming a ritual, a way to meditate *en plein air*.

en plein air (n.) the act of painting outdoors, as opposed to in a studio

mediplair (v.) to meditate *en plein air*, on bike, or foot, as opposed to meditating indoors, eyes closed

véloclair (adj.) the feeling of peace and tranquility while meditating on a bike, in the same rhythm of nature

véloplair (v.) to meditate en plein air, on bike

Oh after I died I hoped the French would coin a word for me. *Véloclair, medivélo, véloplair*, something like that. If I couldn't ever be a songwriter, at least there'd be some legacy.

As I mediplaited, I was weaving past wine bottles, broken fragments, wrapping paper. Sweaters dried out over picket fences. On one street, drag queens on the porch, with their wigs off, in rocking chairs, cigarettes smoked.

Their glances, the ash, it made me think harder about the choices we made. With Kajsa, it was choosing between types of love, love of self versus love of others, friends, siblings.

I passed the cemetery. Huge gravestones were dedicated to aunts, cousins, children. I still didn't understand. Why was a partner the most important relationship of our lives? There was enough evidence, enough living proof — that we had other feelings, other stories, besides what was presented in mainstream film, in pop music, in daily conversation, yet we were so drowned by it, the tidal force was perhaps too big to override. If your twenties and thirties weren't consumed with the right type of relationships, you were focusing on the wrong things. If your twenties and thirties didn't end in marriage, you were an outsider.

Just beyond the soil, a house. A woman shouted, at a child. I was about to cross into its path —

«No, watch it,» she said.

I halted my bike. Tire marks, red.

«You being careful?» she said.

«Sorry,» I said.

«The goat boy,» she said.

«What?» I was confused how she knew that.

«The boy who buys all my goat,» she said.

«Oh my god, Ini,» I said.

Ini chuckled.

«I'm just teasin'.

You barely eat a thing.»

I grabbed my little bicep, embarrassed. I knew I wasn't a jock, but still.

The little boy grabbed at Ini's hip.

«Who's this?» he asked.

Ini shooed him away.

«You want more?» Ini asked.

«Sorry?» I said. I didn't realize she was talking to me.

«Goat,» she said. «I got some stewing.»

«No, no that's okay. I should —

«You don't say no to my goat.

Now you say no.»

«No, yes.»

Ini dangled me, and I was relenting.

She led me through her cottage, to the kitchen. Bright green herbs were piled everywhere. Scotch bonnet peppers, the crimson kind, and bananas.

A huge cast iron Dutch Oven was the stovetop, like a chandelier, the statement piece. The goat was bubbling. Ini opened the lid, the steam emanating. She grabbed a bowl, and ladled a bit of curry onto some rice.

I pulled up a chair. She stood as I tasted.

«It's delicious,» I said.

«Mm,» she said.

I looked around. The sunlight, the stove, they flew in harmony, heat a smooth wind current. Ini rested up against the counter, at ease.

«You live here,» I said.

«Why, yes,» she said. «Do you?»

«No, it's your house.»

«No, yes.» She glanced at me. «In Provincetown.»

«My first time here,» I said.

«Your first season,» she said.

I couldn't lie. I was tired of lies.

«No, I haven't found work. Don't think I can call it a season till I do.»

Ini grabbed a bite of curry. She ladled it the same way, but added a bit of fresh herbs.

«Been here back and forth now, seven years.»

«From Jamaica,» I said.

«Why, yes.»

«Why here?»

Ini looked away. She paused for a moment.

«Some songs,» she mumbled.

«Some one?» I thought I misheard.

She got up to the other room, a slow amble across the kitchen. She returned, with a disc.

«My first album,» she said. It was a picture of her on the album, much younger, singing.

«Can you sing?» I asked.

«Right now, no. Eat your goat.»

I couldn't get an answer, as much as I wanted it. She was someone who was like me, I think. She just wanted to sing while everyone else wanted a weapon. Something to label us as, to make it easier to accept that we were different. By accept, I mean reject.

«I was a background singer,» Ini said.

«Had a chance, one moment. One album.»

I looked up.

«Are you an alto?»

«Soprano,» Ini said.

I turned to stare, but she looked away. Curiosity, I think, it always hurt me.

«How about your friend stops by tomorrow,» she said.

«For real?»

«For real,» she said. «She can paint it.»

Ini turned away, to put away some of the goat. I had convinced her!

As her back was turned, I sneaked her album into my backpack. If she was going to let me paint, why, what was stopping me to help her with other things. I'd convince her to sing, too!

If she didn't mind, that is, letting me borrow a bit of her music. I needed an air of inspiration.

26.

The blue plum sky blazed above as I biked over to Ini's with two buckets in hand, two types of green. From what I was reading on Wikipedia, the Jamaican green was quite a distinct color. It could be achieved by a precise mixing of blue and yellow, like my teacher told me in elementary school, or high school in my case, since art became an elective and lost as power became self-serving love. So I brought a little bottle of blue and yellow, just in case the buckets of green were not the right green, when green painted over the green Ini had on the building resulted in a bitter green.

«Hey Ini,» I said.

«What's this?»

«Got the buckets!» I held them up above my shoulders, like Atlas. «My friend couldn't make it.»

«You promised me a painter.»

«I can paint it.»

Ini put a hand on her apron.

«Mm,» she said.

Ini held up a twenty dollar bill. «Paint till green dries up.»

I got to work on the boutique, dipping a brush into gloops of cold liquid. I swiped the paint across the old green wood and after two hours, were covered, tense and red-handed with effort.

The tense feeling brought my hands back to Bordeaux, and the grapes. France was Jamaica, and Jamaica was France, as long as the United States didn't get in the way, or rather, me not getting in the way of attaching negative feelings to memory. I started to truly believe that people understood certain locations, or didn't, based on color memory. Like if the color of American money, so green, was not as green as Jamaican green, or if the value of green money got so intense that the translucent skin of green grapes didn't look just like wine, but profit. Maybe that's what I saw, but Marie couldn't. And maybe that's why certain relationships were favored, because we couldn't handle the attachments to new colors and humidities. Nostalgia's too sweet. Too damp.

«What'd you do?» Ini asked.

«I'm done?» I asked.

She looked at the zig zag bruises of color, and laughed.

«This isn't good at all. Re-do it.»

I held a piece of ackee in a paper towel, careful to not get it green. Its mild flesh sunk into me.

«Good look on ya,» Luca said.

I looked up at and there he was on his bike. He had a strange clip on his belt.

«Mm?» I said.

«Whatever's on ya,» he said. At first I thought he was making fun of the green all over me, but then I could feel the chunks of fruit between my teeth, and its juice dripping all over my body. I must've looked like a rabid dog.

«Finishing a bit of laundry,» he continued. «If you're done being Jamaican, maybe when I finish we can head to the beach.»

I looked at him when he said that. His eyes, a faded green.

He put on his jacket, getting ready to leave.

I threw out my ackee and opened my backpack. I approached Ini.

«I thought it might look good in here.»

She looked at my hands, a painting.

«A painting?»

«It's my friend's.» I had brought Foska's miniature artwork with me.

Ini held the painting in her hands, and watched as Luca sped away from the porch.

27.

I had biked home to shower off all the green when Luca texted me.

«On my way, be outside,» he wrote.

I ran downstairs quickly, no wallet or phone, ready. I hoped this was something I didn't need to photograph. And gosh how I missed a downstairs rush. Here in the hospital it's only one floor.

Luca arrived on his moped, dangling an extra helmet.

«Before the beach, a little trip,» he said.

I placed my hands around his hips. He turned on the ignition and as we sped through the roads it made a rustling noise, the sound of small tires whistling, protected by tall maples and cottage foliage.

Provincetown was similar to a tiny Greek island, where mopeds roamed like chickens. Despite modern pressures, the town still had space for small tires, grazing across the coastline as we reached the forest trail.

«Is that Foska's blood?» he asked. He dismounted the moped and pointed towards my foot.

«No, god no,» I said.

«From the cassis,» he said. «That's right.» He smiled, I didn't.

For a fall day it was quite warm, short shorts and t-shirt weather still, probably the last breath of verdantry. Emerald branches glittered against a pair of yellow leaves.

«Sassafras,» he said. He stared at the inscription in front of the tree. He traced the word, underlining it with his index finger.

«The original root beer,» I said. I expected a response, but was learning he wasn't as obsessed with food and drink as I assumed. A strange Italian, between the U.S..

We ambled through the trail, the pale brown leaves carpeting the path, the heat of summer still around us, and a view of the lake, dappled with reds and oranges, godlike blue clouds, light that darted through the trees at random intervals which kept its identity moving, not countryside but rural, not beach town but of course not urban. It was the reserves of the Earth breathing several seasons simultaneously.

«I feel my power here,» he said. «In forests.» I nodded. The presence of his observation was fleeting, like the thin stalklike branches in the marshes, wispy enough to fade from vision, but still, phantom energy that kept me wondering how much emotional progress or little thereof I had made. Whether I had forgotten my own experiences. Whether I had tried too many professions and styles of living for one lifetime, that it was too much of a lie to think that in America you could be anything you wanted to be. With all my lies I was missing myself.

He led me towards the dock, thin planks of pebble wood that expanded the view from trail to forest. The entire forest reflected itself in the water, and I was somewhere else. He dipped his feet in, a Provincetown local, fearless in nature and with his body. I leaned against him, and he told me his life story, first in Italy, and then the U.S., for a Master's in Engineering. I didn't realize that in Italy not everyone went to the same type of high school, he in fact, went to a math and science high school, which didn't mean he didn't take art classes, but for four or five years he specialized in subject material, whereas I had just studied everything, even at university, where even specializing in a degree didn't mean I was bound to just that type of coursework. I'd think after an espresso or two I'd approach this subject, or I'd ask that the first time I had met him, but perhaps that was the stereotype I imposed on a foreigner. I didn't consider his past, I considered where he was now. I was just as terrible and miseducated as the ignorant.

We left the dock, necks hanging, regret mid-air. The air of regret, in Frenchspeak.

«Oh I don't want to leave,» he said. «This could be the last of the season.»

There was a lot I didn't know about Luca still. I just hoped it wouldn't be our last moment.

We hopped on the moped and without counting minutes we floated towards his house, where Foska was reclining, taking in a bit of sun, not a care in the world.

28.

We settled on a spot of sand with a view of a boat, sharing a large red blanket. The blue plum sky turned a brighter turquoise.

«What's it like being a Townie?» I asked.

I was hoping Luca was going to say something profound.

«It's... it's close to paradise.»

«Paradise?» I said.

«No other place I'd be.»

«Well, that's quite a statement.» It felt like the wrong town to quote biblical language.

«I mean... can't have everything. Where else can you love like this?»

«Love like what?» I was beginning to think he was less and less Italian.

«Why are you so adversarial?» he asked.

«I'm not.»

«You are.»

«I'm not. Paradise is something only you can dream of.»

«Where else can you love like this?»

«Love like what?» I asked.

«C'mere,» he said. He grabbed my hand.

He pointed to the beach plums, the dunes, the salt watercolors. «Paradise,» he said, surveying.

«I've never lived somewhere, where you can just run into people,» he said. «And run into people like you.»

«Right,» I said. I wasn't sure what to say.

«Italy was like that,» Luca said.

I wished I had known Luca earlier, because he was saying things I never thought to question. For so long it was assumed my life was predetermined.

«Italy was like that,» he repeated.

«In flashes.»

«My mother, my father.»

«Neighbours on the street.»

I nodded.

«It's a small market here, in town.

But there, big big markets.

Walnuts, roasted meats.

Sandwich trucks - tripe -

«Tripe?» I said.

«Eh... intestines.»

«What? Gross.» I pushed him aside, but he leaned against me, laughing.

«It's good,» he said. «Street food. It reminds me of Giulia.»

«Ghoulia,» I said.

He laughed, correcting me, his scruff against my thigh, drawing each letter, a G, then an i, until I felt it. «Giulia. My first friend.»

In the sand I started to sketch a K. Maybe it was okay to keep someone alive. Luca let himself remember the good memories.

«Have you ever loved someone?» he asked.

I looked at the sky, now like a strobe light. Paled turquoise, coral, hot pink taffy. No sirens in sight, just a Provincetown dusk.

From my pocket, I pulled out a thread of Kajsa's sweater.

«Why is she... why does someone have to be the most important relationship of our lives?»

I held the thread, rubbing it between my fingers.

«What is this constant pressure on yourself?»

Luca had tried to intervene.

«You know I used to obsess over someone like that.»

For so long I've tried to develop a theory that it didn't strike me that someone else was figuring out something just as unusual. I wondered if he knew her like I did.

«But then I realized... maybe it was just time to move on from people who couldn't help us anymore?»

vingt-neuf.

After lunch, I had stolen one of the girl's blue lipsticks. The tube had laid on my pillow and before I went to bed I smeared Bye on my wall.

It was time for another bye. A very bad bye.

Last night I snuck into a stranger's apartment. After the phone call with Marie, I think I knew her and I were over. At that point maybe I didn't know, but now I knew it was the right decision.

The door was ajar and I didn't want to go back to the countryside but I had nowhere to sleep, I figured it was safer than homelessness and hypothermia. And it was a new way to look at love. If you were by yourself, no one could hurt you.

The place seemed empty, but at 7:00 am, I heard a man enter. The front door opened and I pretended to be asleep on the sofa, under some blankets. The blue of his nurse costume flitted past me, like the sky was his suit, the atmosphere lowered to the level of the apartment. I had kept my eyes half open as he proceeded to the alcove kitchen. He took the kettle to boil tea. He dropped some loose peppermint into a white porcelain mug. It had Russian letterings. For that ten minute window, he stumbled around, probably searching for food, a banana, some muesli. The water then hummed, him pouring what only looked from my view like fog. He dipped his fingers into the mug just briefly, and then patted the peppermint water on his face. He inhaled the steam, the mix of his cigarettes fading.

«Let's fry it!» Kajsa shouted.

Her stove always had one cast iron pan there, she said for me, so we could try whatever. She sliced the pineapple we had bought, dipping pieces in mustard. We joked about flavouring oils, just smash the seeds and smash the stress!

I pictured this nurse with Kajsa, her arms around him, flicking tea at his face. They were laughing and the fog from the window hazing my view. Another reality hit, someone in her life besides me. I sighed, grabbing my phone, seeing a flight alert. A shit sigh. Somewhere in the middle of the night I had booked a flight home, or maybe drunk, yelling, I demanded a hotel receptionist to do it for me but no, maybe I just wanted an excuse to leave. Four texts ignored from Marie and three missed calls, exclamation points, question marks, nothing I wanted to answer. I had to leave, I think. It was the choice between Marie and Kajsa.

Before the nurse could see me I slipped by, ready for the morning. I couldn't speak to him, it reminded me of Kajsa, when she went on new dates and left me behind. I closed the apartment door, and stumbled two flights down to the entrance. I could barely make out the mosaic on the tiles, it looked like a face of some famous author, or painter, or something like that.

«It's Victor Brodeur,» she said.

There was a woman at the entrance, she had a large gray overcoat on, and a strange hat. It had a sapphire on top. I wanted to leave but I liked her style. It could've been Kajsa's mother. Was it, even?

«Pardon?» I asked.

«You kids these days,» she said. She held onto the wall near the mailboxes. «He was a famous tailor. This was a working class neighborhood, he lived here. He embroidered all the jackets and shirts of the famous politicians, the mayors, the administration staff.»

«Embroidered with what?» I said. I looked at my phone and I still had many hours before I had to catch my plane.

The woman took off her hat. She placed it on the railing.

«Mostly their names, their initials, but some of them had mythical figures, you know, manticores, griffons, that sort. It was a measured honor, if I could say, of how to distinguish yourself. It wasn't fashion, it was how these people lived with themselves, their shame.»

«But the mosaic,» I said. «Wouldn't a carpet, or, I don't know, a framed suit be more appropriate?» It felt a little stiff, talking about shame.

«He was shot,» she said. «Into pieces, it was rumoured. Thus a little joke you could say.» I didn't see the joke, since it felt like she was talking to me about her daughter, my Kajsa.

«I think I would like to die like that too, have my death apparent by the way I died. God forbid someone pocketed me on the street, you know how old I am, you see, so slow, there's no way I could catch up to the robber. But perhaps I fell, slipped, onto the sidewalk. I would like my gravestone to be laid flat too, a little hint of my story. Wouldn't it be nice to know a little more how we died?»

I trotted down the last steps of stairs and nodded, thinking yes.

«No one cares how your daughter died.»

God forbid this actually was Kajsa's mother. It wouldn't be something I knew to handle. It was enough negotiating with one person's memory.

I uttered bad day, quickly stepping into the street, into a market. I saw a police officer, but I couldn't place it. This I remember from once before, where oysters piled up on ice, stubbly radishes next to dark red radishes, and hiding behind them, a little plate of fine bone porcelain with a block of butter, like a gold bar. The market, where I ran after Kajsa.

«Stop!» she said. She was bleeding, or was it me, drops of red liquor.

«If you make me do this, I will report you.» I texted Marie that, my threat. Of course, I could not go back to the vineyard, and she could not make me, now that I knew and now that I had reported her. But my visa was attached to her. Marie had accelerated the process because of all the accounting work I did. She had a friend in the regional Gironde department, and he wrote some special clause that said if I chose to renounce the work I would not be able to find a job in, in France, in Italy, in Germany, no, in all of Europe, because of the special conditions of my agreement. I wondered once if Marie was joking but I had Claudette read the clause for me and yes, it was true, my agreement was sealed. She had political friends, and to think of it, if one could write in a condition, what's to say she didn't have other of these friends. Inspector General Mauriac must've been one too.

I had no choice but to leave and get the hell out of the country.

30

I stood over my kitchen stove, thinking about Luca's observations. Yes, I would move forward.

In the pan, the colors of melted saffron and gorgonzola, the sunset glow of Provincetown. In my mind, the horizon was bloodier.

Foska sneaked into the apartment, raincoat slipping to the floor. Despite the torment, things like this I started to appreciate about her, about my new life. Like here I was, cooking in the kitchen and I could be interrupted. Like Marie and the sunflower oil.

Foska tapped the saucepan.

«Looks tasty,» she said.

«Yah,» I said. Maybe I'd poison her. She opened a bottle, and we cheered.

We started to talk about the cycle, of work, of seasons, how not many people stayed in Provincetown year round, yet after Labor Day it was the first question someone asked, as if the answer wasn't obvious.

«You know,» she started. «The seventeenth time someone asked me 'how long will you be here for?' I said in an older voice, again, 'I don't know.'»

She could imitate the town's voices.

«And then again, a follow up question, the same question, asked by someone different 'will you stay the winter?' and I said, in a child's voice, 'I don't know, I don't think so,' a little different answer, no? and then the follow of the follows, 'but where will you go?' and yeah, I don't know!»

«Can't you just tell the truth?» I asked.

«Huh?»

«That this place, like most places now, is unaffordable, a fantasy land for the select few, thus wroughts the majority of us higher rates of mental illness?»

«That wasn't my point,» Foska replied.

«No, it's mine.» I took a gulp. «We're not helping each other.»

Foska pretended to cheer her glass, as if to prove otherwise.

«Our family,» I said.

«Uh, hello, I live next to my family.»

«When's the last time you did something new?»

Foska was silent.

«That's a ridiculous question.»

«Have you tasted goat?»

«What?»

«Have you tasted goat?» I repeated.

«That has nothing to do with anything.»

«Do you realize how much what you taste matters?»

«That I taste.»

I looked at the clock. 19:01.

«You don't taste something new, heck you don't even try to be a painter because 'you can't stop momentum.'»

Foska scooted back from her chair.

«I'm —

«You're insecure,» I said. «You're - whenever you're around me, you're eating. Around Luca, you're eating.»

«I —

«You're —

«Why couldn't 've you just told me to move on?»

I turned off the burner.

«I was adopted.»

«No one gave a shit about me, and all I read about was happily ever after.»

«With a girl. Which is fine, but all I ever wanted —

«Was a guy.»

«No shut up you idiot.» I paused, and considered my words.

«I met this girl who was the whole reason why I started making music again. Because everyone said we had to get married and had kids and I bet you if you saw anyone by their thirties without kids or without a lover you'd think they were crazy. But I was the least crazy person there was, I was happy with just a sister as my only one. But she died, because of me. And now I have no one.»

Timelines had to be linear, progress instantaneous.

Everyone wanted to feel comfortable, instead of curious. I uncurled the blue lipstick and wrote it all over the wall.

«Do you know why you're fat?»

Foska looked straight at me.

«Because you don't want to deal with your feelings.»

Foska grabbed her raincoat, and walked out of the apartment.

I returned to the stove, adding saffron, and as it swirled downwards it deepened the glow. First scarlet, then crimson, tinted cassis.

I plated it at the dinner table. I tasted it alone, set for me, Foska, and Luca.

31.

The next morning I was still drunk.

I was at the breakwater. It was a clear ocean day, but it felt like a blurry salt froth. I was stumbling on the rocks, singing a little melody. Tourists walked by, turning their heads for a moment, then grabbing their children's hands. Just like the airport, I think. I think I knew why now.

«Thought was one thing, murder was another,» I sang.

As I continued to experiment with random melodies, skipping over wet rocks, chatting with the crabs and the sea gulls, morning turned to afternoon, to dusk.

«She's just jealous!» I shouted into the sunset.

«Super, super jealous.»

Foska had arrived.

«You selfish fuck!»

I peered out, but returned to my melody. They always appeared at the wrong damn time, just when I was composing my best work. I penciled a note onto a shell, then erased it.

«I'm sorry,» I said.

«Oh piss off. You're a mess.»

I laughed. She got me bloody Brit now.

«We're worried about you.» She thought I was pathetic, bitter, and unstable.

«No one's worried about me.»

«You actually are the idiot.» She paused, reconsidering.

«We are worried, we are. I promise.»

And then Luca arrived on his moped. God this was like a film, they should have this film here. After we get our lunch they should prescribe us a film! Kids it's 12 o'clock time for a good show, featuring the breakwater, with a special guest.

«Jeppe, c'mon!» Luca shouted.

«This is all a front!» I said.

I pointed to some tourists, their faces gaped.

«They don't actually care!»

«Jeppe, dude,» Luca said.

I dribbled another melody. Sea gulls squawked.

«What do you think, guys! I'm finally gonna get a recording contract, huh.»

For a second I wondered how they got here, but of course Foska reminded me it was a small town. Didn't I know by then, word travels. People just wanted to help.

I tightened my jacket.

«The music's good, isn't it.»

«Amazing,» Foska said.

«Oh shut up Foska.»

I sat down on one of the giant rocks, still shivering.

«It's not what I think, it's what you think.»

«Are you actually sorry or just drunk?»

My fingers, bloody from the barnacles, when I tried to do a handstand earlier that afternoon. Bloody and blue, too, from the cold. Luca passed me his jacket. I refused, but he put it over my shoulders.

«I'm sorry,» I said. «I just don't know how to do this.»

I think at this point I started to realize the extent of my confession, but it wasn't the song, or the jacket, or Foska, or any of them really by themselves. It was them cumulatively, the fact that it wasn't just one person who could help me. They all helped me. I think to let go, help needed to be not just yourself or someone else, but a whole lot of people. Three, to start.

«Foska's just stubborn,» Luca said.

«I'm not stubborn. Apology accepted.»

There was probably at least ten tourists watching over us now. A police car in the front, with sirens.

«No I mean, I just don't know if I can do this, here.»

Foska thought I was talking about the breakwater, and the tourists watching.

«Don't be ridiculous. We can just walk right past them.»

«Since when do you make decisions?» Luca asked.

«Guys I have to tell you something.»

«Can't it wait?»

«N-no. It's important.»

«It can wait until the morning.» Foska looked at Luca.

«Yeah, you're one good lookin' dude right now.»

Luca nodded at me, and we all overlooked the breakwater, tourists still staring, police siren still flashing, but all I noticed was the three of us. I had let go.

«How about we hit the beach in the morning? And then we talk. Jeppe you can tell us everything.»

«Okay.»

«I got it,» Foska said. «Let's rent some dune cars.»

«Tomorrow?»

«Yeah I'll take off work.»

«You've skipped like three shifts this week.»

«It's fine, it's not like —

«I killed her.»

«Huh?»

I stared back at the tourists.

«When I said she died, because of me. I left out that I killed her.»

«Okay we get it, you're sorry. Let's move on.»

«I am moving on.»

I looked once more at the breakwater, the salt froth, the blue plum sunset.

«I... I need to go to the police.»

«The hell are you talking about? You're not actually insane, I was kidding earlier.»

They say let go but I look at the sun and argue, it doesn't go, it just rises and falls. It continues. If nature does not go, why must I?

That was the last thought, before I told them my more storied truth in detail.

trente-deux.

«*Sucré ou salé?*» the flight attendant asked. Sweet — or salty
—

I had gotten on the plane with my phone still buzzing, Marie
calling, one last plea, the other flight attendants asking if I was
alright. I was wearing rain boots.

I looked at the cart. The snacks were in steel bins.

«What're the ingredients?» I said.

«What?» the attendant said.

I craned my neck and scanned the list. Olive oil, wheat flour,
salt. A simple recipe with three ingredients, not like home, with
forty. I was wondering if this was my last chance to be free.

«*Salé,*» I said.

The flight attendant placed the crackers down on my tray,
and marched on to the next person.

«*Sucré ou salé?*»

I got up to walk around, turning to see huge smiles. A hulk-
woman, and her two colleagues, middle school teachers on a
school trip to Boston. They stood in the flight attendant bar area,
dress shirts and pants but slouching like zombies, drained by the
forty children on board.

I tried to chat to them, but it was three in the morning. No
one had time for small talk at this point.

After they left, I loitered.

An elderly man approached me.

«Beautiful country,» he said.

«Ah yes,» I said. I turned to the lavatory.

«The culture's just so so different,» he said.

«Mm,» I said. He stepped a little closer, to hold onto the bar counter where the flight attendants kept the coffee pots.

We stood in silence.

«That woman you saw,» he said, pointing at the aisle, «she's not my wife.»

I said nothing, thinking many things.

«Her husband died last month of cancer,» he said. «As did my wife, same time, also cancer.»

I looked at him, thinking to say I'm sorry, or something awkward, but said nothing. I kind of liked that someone else was struggling with the definitions of loved ones.

«She was my wife's roommate,» he said. «Dream of all of ours to go to France. Guess we did. Do you have someone like that?»

«My sister,» I said.

«Your sister, you have the hots for your sister?»

«It's not like that,» I said, furious. «She died. Well, kind of. It felt like she died.» I turned away, playing with one of the Air France napkins.

«No worries, kid.» I thought he was trying to give me a piece of advice. First, don't fall in love with your sister. Second, go to France, that'll solve everything.

I looked at my rain boots, noticing the dried dirt, and feeling on the inside, under my sock, a vine twig.

«It's nice here,» I said.

«I'd stay if I could,» he said.

I stopped listening. I thought maybe death would've taught him, but in fact it was me who I think was learning. I was dreaming of something that I wanted to return to, like maybe a Jamaican would, except, it felt like I was returning to a hurricane's tomb. I was going to confess my crime, even if others wanted to do it for me, or erase its value. That was the truth of my situation, that even institutionalised people had fog to bleed. I thought I'd be trapped forever if I didn't set it all loose, all of France's precipitation, all of my own detective work. You see, I admit all this from a psych ward, but I'd only become crazy later, after I retraced my steps, and realized I was destined to leave France. I was and always would be an American, my crimes uniquely this country's. I was not crazy but creative, not normal enough unless it was quickly digestible sugar thinking and it took a distortion of time to decant that simple truth.

33.

I realized that I just had to murder my thoughts, before the thoughts were formed, like clouds into rain.

As clouds, water could drift backwards, back into cotton candy. Words and thoughts were actions, it's just the thoughts had to be restrained, limited like sweets I couldn't act upon.

I know. I should be happy I'm able to recall this level of specificity, that I can be sorry, that some people are still alive, still breathing, that I bet somewhere this confession is in some drawer with the rest of my notes. This story and the fall leaves, quivering together, this was post-Provincetown triage.

Bloody hands it was me. I was staring at the photo Luca gave me. It was a picture of me at the crime scene, years younger. I thought I had aged little but it was just the Cape fading my innocence. A lot of information to process, a lot of help offered to me. Luca really was a cop, but that's not how I was treated. Attached to the photo was the name of a psychiatrist.

I meant to say earlier that Ini drove me out of town, to check me in. The least she could do, she said, for the decent paintwork. I guess yeah, that was a pretty good paint job wasn't it. I told Ini c'mon, forget your restaurant, we should try to sing the season's emotions, the fall, its vinaigrette sunlight. We were going to write a song that said as long as we were honest, bitter and sweet could coexist, just add salt, or winter, we just had to admit, I—

«Hi Jeppe! I'm in Los Angeles, are you around?»

I glanced at my phone to see a message from Marie. Mind you I didn't live in Los Angeles, or 3,000 miles near it. But close by I remembered the grand tour she gave me when I first got to Bordeaux, the wine bottles, the yellow glass and the Atlantic, the sauntering July. She was tall, with shovels, and now sweet, messaging me.

From my new ward I was watching *Les Diaboliques*, a 1955 black and white French film. I'd think of Marie and then the clap clap clap of the school, *les enfants*, the *«je te jure,»* the English teacher «to give,» «to want,» «to get,» cascading verbs, stumbling on «to dream.» I wondered why Marie thought to message me. I thought about scrolling through all the contacts in my phone. If I had messaged even a third of them, what surprises would I get?

The pool water, the drowned body, that provoked the teacher's cœur that claqued, for me, it was the bottle of brandy, gated memories of decanted wine, sediments of 1987, the children my memories filing back inside.

«Qu'est-ce que j'ai?» she's asking them. What do I have? What do I have. She ambled towards the swimming pool, and not seeing what she buried, she fainted. My body was missing.

I could message her. I'd go back to Bordeaux, she'd invite me to her son's wedding, I'd stay, an American accent thickening amongst an inflection.

Histoire de fou, a history of crazy. The two teachers were shouting at each other, she was crazy to listen to her. I was a teacher too. I was replacing them with me, at least one of them.

I was shouting at myself, wondering what I should do next but locked in here. God this film was so much better when I adapted it to my situation.

The body of Luca was missing too. My friend in the forest, he had left me in Provincetown.

Simple things brought me back to here, 1955. The porter of *boulanged* goods, the soft rolls, the croissants, the long cut chocolate within. What if in my elementary school there was a porter like that, a snack break of ringing bells and pastries.

«Go ahead, call the police, what're you waiting for?» I'll confess. No, they'll see the newspaper, a body found in the Charles. She'll go to the morgue. In the undertunnels the staff will search for the right box, they'll pull her out. I wondered if it could be my body of former years and memories.

A photograph of what looks like Foska, with a wood racquet. The detective flipped over the photograph to write a report, interrupted by the chattering of children my memories.

«Ra ta ta ta!» they shouted, mimicking a gun. «Ra ta ta ta!»

Jeppe Jeppe Jeppe

Jeppe on the typewriter

She had never died, it was his mind the directrice who suffered, a fragile heart.

No Marie, I was not in Los Angeles, I was traveling with Ini.

The 42 bus line was known as the Druid. We waited for it under the tunnel, a puddled two way street where Boston dignitaries and transit folk all convened. Ini was dropping me off at the hospital.

I looked up to spot a woman in her Mazda. Traffic had pushed us all together, the cars hadn't moved for three or four minutes. For whatever reason, her eyes caught me, the blue green fogginess of sea glass, the way they angled down, glinting as the sharpest of the tunnel lights. She looked at me. It was Kajsa.

What she was doing, what we were all doing in this damp tunnel going somewhere, because we all had somewhere to be, why I had decided to take the bus at seven twenty seven in the morning.

As she pressed the gas pedal I couldn't say what was within.